A CAT'S TALE OF HEARTACHE AND MISERY

KATIE WARREN

THE TUNA FISH DIARIES: A CAT'S TALE OF HEARTACHE AND MISERY.

For information address wildonepress@outlook.com

First Edition

Published by Wild One Press

Cover Art by Govina Taylor
Formatting by Dianna Roman

ISBN: 978-1-959553-09-0 (Trade Paperback)
ASIN: B0CGGTL36V (ebook)

DEDICATION

To my dad—
here is a book you can read.

To my husband—
who wanted Fishsticks to have his own book more than I did.

To the actual Fishsticks—
who is nothing like this... yet.

And to the readers of *The Right Wrong Number*—
you asked, and I delivered. This is for you.

AUTHORS NOTE

Even though it may look like it, this book is not appropriate for children.

I started writing this for the fans of Fishsticks in *The Right Wrong Number* and it very quickly took on a life of its own. You won't find this to be powerful or moving, in fact, you'll probably find this utterly ridiculous. But I hope it makes you laugh, because that's the whole point.

Note: This can be read as a standalone. You do not need to read *The Right Wrong Number* to enjoy Fishsticks' story.

CHAPTER 1

Fishsticks

Dear Diary,

I think that's the proper way to address you, but I am not sure, as I have never done this before. Apparently, I need to get my emotions out in a constructive manner because I have been feeling very unwell as of late. I am trying very hard not to take my feelings of displeasure out on the human in my enclosure but that man, Jules, is beyond difficult to reside with. So, Diary, that is why I am utilizing you, to help serve the greater good of the humans' existence. I promise to do my best not to terrorize the human in this household by expressing my feelings adequately. Even though I am a feline with a very high I.Q., I cannot make any promises.

Things have been distinctively unusual in my domain recently, and I cannot put my paw on it. The humans have not been following their normal mundane routine. And my human, James, has been gone for several sunrises. He did not say farewell to me by taking his travel device out of his closet before he left. I have learned that this is the way my human says goodbye and makes me aware that he will be absent for a prolonged period of time. When my human does this activity, I know he will leave me with the repugnant human, Jules, so I attempt to lay inside of it in protest. But none of these things have occurred which leaves an intelligent cat like myself, mystified.

Why did my human leave without his travel device? I am very worried for him. He is not supposed to leave for this long without his travel device! Oh, James, what have you done? I hope you are okay out in the wild without it.

To make matters worse, the human that I greatly dislike, Jules, has been overly problematic for these past few sunrises and quite frankly, I am exasperated by him. All that incomprehensible man has done is leak water down his face and make horrid shrieking noises that are much too loud for my sensitive cat ears to handle. His ungodly noises are interrupting my very essential sleep schedule. Does he not realize how loud he is? My job as a professional napper takes dedication, and the only way my task will be achieved is if he shuts the fluff up. Doesn't he realize being a professional napper is not an easy job? And God forbid he actually leave his bed! I must pry him out with my scratchers in order to get a decent meal around here. If he does not want to leave his bed, he should have an ounce of common sense and leave me several meals in my bowl at one time, then let me gorge them all at once. But this human makes absolutely no sense at all, and it is absolutely maddening.

Also, Nora, the witchy woman who reeks of puréed grasses has been making more appearances in my domain than necessary. I have tried to get her to understand that she needs to leave by charging at her feet with my daggers when she enters my enclosure, but that vile woman has not picked up on my nonverbal cues. I will have to manipulate my strategy to make her understand how I really feel about her.

Speaking of that mindless human, here she comes, stomping through my enclosure like she owns the place. This is my house! Who does she think she is?

I must go now, as I have essential activities to attend to. This time, I will attempt to get ahold of the tail that is always hanging from the back of her head with my sharp teeth. Does she not know that tails should come from the back of your body and not the top? And she just swings it around, taunting me with it. She is so obtuse and illogical, and I will not even try to understand her abnormal habits.

How dare my human leave me for this long! This is utterly neglectful! Maybe if I meow very loudly at the door, he will hear me? I shall try that tactic and see if it summons him back to me.

Oh James, come home soon, I beg of you. I miss your soft lap and soothing cat calls.

The Weekly Catio Report: When I was out on my catio yesterday, I made a chirpy purr of inquiry to Sally the Tuxedo Cat in 2B. Sally calls herself fancy because she wears a tuxedo every day, and even though I don't understand her train of thought, I do agree she is easy on my cat eyes. She told me the story her mother told her of her Great Uncle Henry the Third. She said not to fret over the loss of my beloved human, as her Great Uncle Henry

says that the humans only have one life and felines have nine lives. This means the humans will come and go from our lives because we are the superior species. Even though I agree with her Great Uncle Henry's assessment, it does not make my heart any less weary.
I will be sure to make a chirpy purr of inquiry to Chuck Norris the Ragdoll over in 6C to see his thoughts on my predicament.

CHAPTER 2

JULES

Every time you see a funeral in the movies, it's a dreary rainy day, and the wind picks up at just the right time, letting everyone know their loved one is there watching over them. But that's not what James' funeral is like.

No, hc had to make sure it was a perfect North Carolina day. Sunny and mild with no humidity and no sudden breeze to tell me he's here, watching over us.

I'm flanked by my best friend Nora and my mother, one on each side of me. They each hold one of my arms, like they're making sure I don't drop to my knees. I'm not sobbing. I'm not upset. I'm not anything. I'm numb. The only thoughts in my mind are that I'm going to have to be the one who picks up the dry cleaning. I'm going to be the one who feeds the evil cat that is Fishsticks. I'll never see the toothpaste James so stubbornly left behind in the sink. Who thinks about toothpaste during a funeral?

Standing at the edge of his grave, my feet sink into the soft earth beneath me. I stare at his closed casket, but all I see is his face dripping blood behind the wheel of his car. All I hear is screeching and honking, the last sounds James heard. Even though I never saw any of it, even though I wasn't even there, my mind makes up what it could have been, what it probably was.

No, I wasn't there to die with him. I was asleep in a dream land, while my husband took his last breath. I was completely unaware that when I woke up my life would never be the same.

Lifting a scoop of dirt in my palms, I shift it around in my hands. Clutching it tightly, I don't want to let it drop. The second this dirt leaves my hands is the second James will cease to exist in any physical sense. Reluctantly,

I throw the soil on top of the pile along with a flower. James didn't have a favorite flower, so I picked whatever Nora suggested. Who thought I would be a thirty-six-year-old man picking out flowers for my husband's casket?

When I turn around, Nora and my mother immediately return to my side. Nora's arm wraps around my shoulders while we slowly walk back to the car. I have nothing to say, nothing of value anyway. What do you say when your husband is dead? I mean, did I miss that course in school? It should be a class in college titled, "What to do When Your Spouse Dies", one-oh-fucking-one.

Getting in the car, I slam the door behind me. Nora has a tissue in her hand, tears streaming down her face.

"I'm so sorry, Jules," she whispers. "I'm so, so sorry."

I tune her out, all I can hear are shovels ringing in the distance. Shovels that are slinging dirt onto my husband, so he's never seen again.

CHAPTER 3

Fishsticks

Daily Cat-ffirmation:

In my sadness, I love myself.

Dear Diary,

My human still has not returned. It has been more sunrises than a cat can count. Although that is a tragedy in and of itself, something far more dreadful has occurred within my enclosure. It is so awful and inconsiderate that I have fallen into a deep state of depression.

The witchy woman, Nora, has brought all her items into my habitat. My humble abode has been filled with her vile decorations and her clothing that reeks of a stomach-churning smell. I have only ever been in the wild on a few occasions, so I am not paws-itive, but I would guess she smells like a floral bouquet and grass. It is utterly appalling. Who would want to smell like the out of doors? Every time I have been out of doors it has been a very unpleasant experience. Who would want to smell like such an awful thing?

James, oh James, why have you left me? Please come back and save me from these humans and this ill treatment that I am enduring. Why James? Why would you do this to your purebred prized feline? We spent almost seven lovely lives together. Now that you are gone, I expect these last three lives to be grueling.

I have been considering this horrible situation and I have decided to form a protest. There is only so much a feline can withstand and this woman has met her match! I jumped on the table and knocked down all her hideous décor with my feather duster. What kind of human would place these atrocious things on every available surface? Doesn't she know that I am king of this domain, and that I will leap onto all the furniture when it pleases me? No, she covers every surface she can with her artifacts. She has gone too far! You would think I would have gotten my point across when I smashed several of her things to the floor which made her shriek at me in incomprehensible tones. But no, she continues to mock me by putting them all back where she placed them previously. The fluffing audacity!

My next tactic is to act like I've forgotten where my sandbox is and urinate in her laundry basket. This will teach her to stop smelling like grassy floral arrangements. I have concluded that she needs to leave immediately. She has messed with the wrong feline.

And to think my human left me with these despicable humans without a whisker of remorse! I must find him as soon as possible. My last resort is to flee my domain to find him out in the wild. I shudder at the thought, but I have a proficient sniffer and I am positive I can track him down. I will meow at the door in an attempt to tell the spare human that I have very important appointments outside. Hopefully these pathetic excuses of human beings will listen to my demands. Free Fishsticks!

I will get to these duties, just after I take my sixth nap of the day.

The Weekly Catio Report: Chuck Norris the Ragdoll in 6C was absolutely no help in solving my crisis. All he would talk about was this brown paper bag he had obtained from his human. I finally went inside my enclosure after he meowed on and on with what felt like hours. I am sorry Chuck Norris, but I have real problems over here and your happiness is insulting to me.

P.S. — The only satisfactory thing that has occurred is the number of empty boxes Nora has left in my habitat. The fact that the human, Jules, never leaves his bed has worked in my favor. If I don't make it out of here and into the wild, I shall be spending my future siestas in a nice inviting box.

CHAPTER 4
JULES

I wake up feeling like my chest was caving in, but that's pretty much the norm now. Breathe in. Breathe out. Breathe in. Breathe out.

I've actually gotten used to having to remind myself to breathe every morning, but this morning it's worse than ever. The grief is still leaking out of me like thick tar. Every day is still a search for how to let it out for fear of drowning in it.

Grabbing my phone off of the nightstand, I see it's 7:56 a.m. It's been one year, six hours, and thirteen minutes since I lost James, although sometimes it feels like just yesterday. One year since that phone call that forever changed my life. The phone call that put a gaping hole in my soul, making me never want to leave this bed again.

Rolling over, I stretch my arms over my head and blink my eyes awake, staring at a room that is no longer James', even though his nightstand still contains all his things. The dresser is still full of his clothes. The light blue paint that he picked out is still on the walls. There are so many memories of him here, but not him. It's both a comfort and a horrid tease. A loud growl from the end of the bed interrupts my depressing observations.

Fishsticks is shooting daggers at me like he might kill me at any moment. Good morning to you too, evil creature.

Fishsticks was James' cat, and he makes it no secret that he despises me. I'm just his personal can opener who he is plotting to kill. A hateful hiss follows his unholy growl, telling me I need to get up and feed him.

"Fuck off, Fishsticks," I mumble, glaring back. I'm bigger damn it. Not by much, but I'm bigger.

He turns around, flashing me his rotund orange ass. This cat will be the death of me. I swear. Murder by cat. And if I do happen to die of natural causes, I don't even want to think about how disrespectful he'll be to my corpse before anyone finds me. Not that there's ever been much love lost between Fishsticks and I, but after I listened to that coroner on one of my true crime podcasts detail how cats have no shame when it comes to snacking on their owners after their demise, I have watched the beast with an even more suspicious eye. I'd better not die at home or there will be nothing left for my mother to bury as long as Fishsticks is in this apartment.

Horrendous noises from the kitchen make my muscles clench. Sighing, I rub my eyes. She's on perfect schedule, the godawful whirling and grinding echoing down the hallway. For the past year, at 8:00 a.m., I've had to hear that damn blender.

"For the love of all that is holy, will you turn that wretched machine off? Eat something greasy for a change! It sounds like you're drilling a hole into my goddamn brain!" I yell at the top of my lungs.

Wait for it. And…here she comes—Nora and her dramatic stomps in 3....2....1...

"I'll tell you what. I'll eat something greasy, if it gets you out of this bed. Get up, wash your ass, and let's go get us some waffles!"

"No," I grunt, covering my face with the pillow. "I'm not in the mood. You know what today is."

My heart feels like it has left my body, and all Nora can think about is waffles? Does she have any decency?

"I've moved into your home and taken care of you for a year. I know you're grieving, but you cannot lie here all day, every day, doing nothing! You think James would want you to live like this? You've barely left this room in a year, and you haven't written a single word since he died. Not. A. Single. Word."

The morning reminder that my corpse will be eaten by Fishsticks one day, the barrage of blender noises like an air raid, and now a painful truth bomb pointing out my lack of productivity. That's it.

"Alright! I'll get some fucking waffles if it makes you shut up," I yell, throwing my covers off and stomping into the bathroom.

She wants waffles? She'll get fucking waffles. I'll even hurry up, shower, and change just to prove I can still function. I might only wash half my ass out of spite.

Nora and I go back to when we were in car seats. She can annoy me to no end with her never-ending antics, her incessant singing, and the weird Post-it notes she leaves all over the house. However, rather than treating me like a piece of fine china after James died, she's never been afraid to tell me exactly how she feels. I think everyone needs their own personal Nora—a loud, obnoxious honesty-button. By the way we endlessly bicker, someone probably wouldn't guess that I actually am grateful to have her. If it weren't for Nora, I'd be a permanent fixture on my mattress. I'd have perished from bedsores and starvation, and then been devoured by Fishsticks, since it's her personal mission in life to make sure I've gotten up and eaten at least twice a day.

Dragging myself to the bathroom vanity counter, I catch a glimpse of my reflection in the mirror. Wow. I see why Nora's been on my case the past six months. How have I not realized how much I've let myself go? There was no reason to look in the mirror. There was no love of my life to impress anymore.

My shaggy brown hair is starting to curl around my ears in a very unflattering way. The blue eyes that James loved so much now house large black bags under them. I scrub my face, feeling a beard that was never there when James was alive. Looking down at my bare torso, I see soft skin. My rock-hard abs have officially disappeared.

God, I look like shit. It's time for this beard to go. I look like a caveman.

Walking out to the living room freshly shaved, I bark, "There! My ass is washed. Now let's get some stupid waffles."

Nora taps the toe of one of her red Converse shoes against the floor, like she's been waiting all day. She's obviously been up way longer than I have. She already has her cat-eye eyeliner painted on her face and is wearing her signature big curls.

"Holy shit! You shaved the beard! Thank The Lord! You were starting to look like you were a member of the Duck Dynasty clan. Also, no offense, but you stunk. I could smell you from the living room. I was considering calling your mother and giving you a shower intervention."

CHAPTER 5

Fishsticks

Daily Cat-ffirmation:

I am the perfect size.

Dear Diary,

It's official: things in this enclosure have gotten out of paw! If I had opposable thumbs, I would call the ASPCA and report these humans for feline cruelty.

I have to do everything in this habitat, and quite frankly, I am sick of it! I must pry that pathetic excuse of a replacement cat dad out of bed just to feed me. The sun may not have risen yet, but so what? Shouldn't a cat be able to eat on his own free will? This is what he gets for feeding me morsels for dinner. I cannot make it through the night without being absolutely famished.

To add insult to injury, I don't think this witchy woman is leaving. How dare that vile man invite other humans to come into my habitat without my permission! Oh Diary, how I despise her. She is sanctioning my kibble! How dare she call me things like fat and obese? I am not oversized, I am fluffy! Does she not realize how much fluff I am carrying around?

I have been spending my days redecorating because that woman is still putting these atrocious knickknacks on every surface. You would think she'd learn by the number of times I've knocked her things down, but no. I've concluded that she is, in fact, brainless. I meowed at her once on a Sunday and instead of doing what I asked she meowed back at me in an angry tone with sixteen grammatical errors. All I did was politely demand that she pull the treats out of my cabinet because I am becoming malnourished, but what do I expect from a human who can't even meow correctly? For fluff's sake!

I have also come to accept the fact my human is not coming back to my enclosure. It has been countless sunrises and he has still not returned. His smell is slowly diminishing from my habitat, so I have kept the one thing that still contains it. It may be a filthy sock, but I do not care. I need it! It's all I have left of him! I shall always keep it close to me, even if his scent diminishes from it with each passing sunset. I dare these humans to try to take it away from me.

Oh, James. How could you do this to me? You rescued me from cat jail all those lives ago! I was just a small feline when you came and saved me from that atrocious imprisonment. Why would you leave me like this? I thought you loved me.

I miss you. Damn it. Now I'm so depressed, I'm even more hungry.

The sun has not quite risen, but I must sign off as it's time to wake up my pathetic excuse for a replacement cat dad.

The Weekly Catio Report: I made a chirpy purr of inquiry to Cheddar, the other orange cat in 3D, on his catio the other day. Even though he is orange like me, I think I am much more handsome than he is. I have a large fluffy tail that acts as a feather duster, where his tail is just scrawny and unsightly. He sat on his catio to do his daily bird watch, and he told me how he has had several humans leave him and he has had several habitats throughout his lives. This makes me wonder if Cheddar is an adequate feline. Why would he be rehomed countless times? Is he a sorry excuse for a feline? I think that I shall not meow at Cheddar anymore. I'm now worried about his integrity as a cat and his guidance to my crisis.

CHAPTER 6

Fishsticks

Dear Diary,

It has been some time since my last entry. Things have been worse than I feared. I have been utterly grief stricken due to my human's disappearance, and my mental health has been on the decline. Sadly, I have spent all my days absorbing photosynthesis and looking out my window (but, as we felines know, looking out the window takes all day if you do it right). I could not bear to do anything but take long naps with James' sock, eat this disgusting dietary kibble, and make strategic plans of how to retaliate against the humans James has left me with.

Things have been absolutely dreadful since my human has disappeared. I have not gotten timely water bowl changes, treats when I meow in the correct tone, appropriate scritches under my chin at my demand, and most of all, Tuna Tuesdays. I have not had a Tuna Tuesday in at least three hundred and sixty-some-odd days! These two humans may have sanctioned my kibble, but how dare they take away my Tuna Tuesdays! How am I supposed to live like this?

Despite the tragic loss of chin scritches, the sweet talking I deserve, and James' ever-inviting lap to curl up on, my misery does not end there. No. Forget the dire loss of one's loving human!

Universe, how you mock me with the added trials you have hoisted upon my nine lives.

I do not know what James ever saw in this Jules. That human's lap is too solid and bony. I find just as much comfort sleeping on the hardwood floor.

Out of pure desperation, I once let him pet me on a Thursday afternoon.

He was scritching all the wrong places, and he had the audacity to pat my butt in a very offensive manner. He forced my paw, and I had to get out my scratchers. And for fluff's sake, he is not the only one who is depressed, yet I must remind him every morning to drag himself out of bed just to provide me with the disgusting dietary fare he and that witchy woman he invited to move in insist I survive on.

Something in my habitat must change or I am going to request that I be rehomed. I have needs and what I need is a Tuna Tuesday! All I ask is for this spare human to crack open a can of tuna. It's a simple request, yet they give me this mediocre kibble for the nine hundredth time. Fluff my lives, why are you so dense NoRaAAa?!

I'm off to meow at my treat cupboard in an attempt to get a proper snack. I see that awful woman eating several snacks during the course of a day and she has yet to offer me one. Why do I have to be on a diet if she doesn't? I do not know if she realizes this, but she has a little junk in her trunk. If anyone needs a proper diet, it is her! I am ravenous. Good fluff, I just need a little pick me up. A few morsels of Temptations never hurt anyone. If my beloved human was here, I would have several snacks a day. I had him trained for both afternoon and evening snack times. As we felines say, dogs have owners, cats have staff. My new staff is unwilling to cater to my needs. After dealing with these atrocious humans, I've come to realize James was the best staff I could ever have. There will never be another James.

Oh, this seventh life is full of misery and heartache.

I apologize for my lack of Weekly Catio Report. I have been too distressed to go out and get a proper sunbath. But I think I need to go out and absorb photosynthesis to combat this depression. I will put a three-hour sunbath on the catio in my catto-planner, along with a good spa session. I need a whole entire day in my kitty condo to catch up on my skin care routine. I will admit this to only you, but my fluff is a mess!

CHAPTER 7
JULES

"Alright, Nora. Let's do this! Where is the beast?" I grumble, walking down the hallway, peering around corners.

This is going to be a fucking nightmare. I feel like I need to wear those chainmail outfits that people wear to those Renaissance Faires in order to get out of this unscathed.

"Don't you dare let him see that thing! Keep it in the hallway!" she yells, gesturing to the crate wildly.

Putting the crate down, I sneak into the living room in stealth mode. The last time James and I attempted to do this; it took an hour. I'm betting it'll take at least two and a trip to the emergency room this time.

"What's your plan of attack?" I ask.

"I stuck some catnip in his food this morning. I'm hoping he'll be so high that he won't notice our covert operation." Nora beams.

"Fat chance. The amount of catnip it takes to make that cat high is obscene," I mutter.

Fishsticks is fast asleep on the couch, snoring, obviously coming down from his buzz. How much catnip did Nora scrounge up? Maybe this won't be as difficult as I thought. I start to sneak up on him, but the floor creaks beneath my feet. He jolts out of his catnip coma and onto all fours like he's ready to rumble.

I knew it. It was too good to be true.

"He doesn't look high," I say, throwing a stink eye at Nora. "In fact, he looks like his normal pissed off self."

Sneaking around to his other side, Nora whispers, "I'm hoping his responses slow down. Like he won't see what's coming until it's too late."

I kneel beside the couch and am greeted with a hiss. Holding my hand out in a feeble attempt to get into his good graces, I soothe, "Hey, Fishsticks. How was your nap, buddy?"

One of his beefy paws swats through the air with the speed of a cheetah. It's so fast, I don't have time to draw back. His sharp claws slice across the back of my hand.

"He got me!" I yank my hand back, staring at the three crimson lines across my flesh.

Just as I let out a yelp, Nora's hand darts under his belly like she's attempting to lift him up while he's distracted over his victory from maiming me. With amazingly not-high cat reflexes, he turns with a loud growl and lunges for her fingers, leaving a cat tooth imprint behind.

"Ow! Fuck you too, Fishsticks!" she screeches, tossing him back on the cushion and grabbing her finger.

Snatching the throw blanket off the couch as Fishsticks arches his back like he's gearing up for WWIII, I blurt, "I have an idea!" Tossing the blanket, I hold my breath as it balloons in a canopy over Fishsticks. His massive form shifts underneath it like he's searching for escape.

Fuck. We only have seconds.

"Grab him! Now!" I command.

Nora bomb dives on top of the blanket, hugging her arms around the Fishsticks-sized lump in the center of it. The throaty growl he emits is no less terrifying than if it weren't muffled by the thread count.

"Get the thing! Get the thing!" she yells at me, while wrestling with the huge lump under her arms.

"What thing?" I flail my arms, trying to figure out what she wants from me. Does she have a tranquilizer gun hidden somewhere as a back-up plan that she didn't tell me about?

"The crate, you idiot!" she grunts, clearly having to use all her strength to subdue James' precious, pissed off pet.

When I scramble back from the hallway with the crate, I hold it up to the edge of the couch cushion and swing open the door. Nora tries to put Fishsticks inside, but just as I told her this operation would end up, that goes to shit too.

"Why...is he...so fucking…fat?" she wheezes.

I don't know who's making more noise: her grunting or Fishsticks' unholy, livid sounds. Damn, he has gotten big. He wouldn't fit into a cat crate, so James and I bought a small dog crate instead, but now even that looks like it's shrunk. When Nora finally helps Fishsticks inside the dog crate, I slam the door shut just as he lashes out toward the opening. I really want to stick his special sock in there for comfort, but I don't dare open the door again for fear of retaliation.

Man, that only took like five minutes. Amazing! Blanket idea for the win! One point for Jules. Zero points for Fishsticks. Finally, I won at something.

"Awesome!" I exclaim as the latch clicks shut. "That was way easier than last time."

Nora picks up the crate with a scowl. "Let's just get this over with," she huffs, attempting to carry the crate in one hand.

Fishsticks is so large and shuffling around in agitation that it sets the whole crate off balance, making it teeter back and forth in her grasp.

"Give him to me," I say, taking the crate from Nora. Her skinny arms clearly can't handle his weight. As soon as she hands him over, the strain of carrying him and the crate tugs my arm down like an anchor, making me shift to one side.

"Holy hell! He's gained way more weight than I thought!" I exclaim.

This crate must weigh at least thirty pounds with Fishsticks inside of it. I did not realize he had gotten this big.

Once Fishsticks is in the car, I almost have hope that this vet visit is going to be easier than I thought. It's only a fifteen-minute drive to the clinic, but the sounds that are coming from the back seat resemble those of a demon straight from hell. Nora turns up the radio trying to drown him out, but Fishsticks just mews louder.

The mix of Nora's dreadful pop music and Fishsticks possessed demon sounds is giving me a headache. As soon as we get in the parking lot, I jab the radio, turning off the music.

"I can't. I can't anymore. If there's a hell, I'm in it right now," I sigh, rubbing my temples.

Getting out of the car, I take the crate out of the backseat and bend over to peer at Fishsticks inside.

"There, there. Don't worry. Even though you hate me, I won't subject you to any more of Nora's singing," I soothe, patting the top of the crate like I'm saving a cat that actually loves me.

*****

There must have been a note in Fishsticks' file about his unsatisfactory behavior at the vet because the man who comes into our room doesn't look like a veterinarian. He looks like Hannibal Lecter. Dr. Theo's thick welding gloves go up his whole arm. Metal mesh gloves for this demonic cat, I can understand. Makes sense. I'll have to try that next time I have to wrangle

Fishsticks, but the mask? Jesus. What happened the last time James brought Fishsticks in that this guy is wearing a freaking welding mask?

"Oh my God, are you a Mandalorian?" I ask him. Glancing at Nora for confirmation, I add, "Is this real life?"

Dr. Theo backs away from the crate and lifts his mask revealing a grimace. "I remember what happened the last time Fishsticks was here. It wasn't pretty. This is…just a precaution. Now, let's try to take him out of the crate, but…slowly please," he adds just before lowering his mask.

Shit. It's bad when even the veterinarian is terrified of your cat.

As soon as I open the door, Fishsticks darts out and stumbles, looking up at me with pure disgust in his eyes.

"Oh, shit," I mutter, slowly inching toward the opposite corner of the room.

"Okay, Doc. He's not losing weight," Nora rushes out like she wants out of this room as badly as I do. "And I've had him on a diet for almost a year. All he wants to do is eat all day and all night. He also drinks so much water that I can barely keep the bowl filled before it's gone. Oh, and he needs his rabies shot updated, too.".

Nora and her whole water issue. My God, it's not rocket science.

"That's because he's obese, Nora. He's thirsty because even walking around the apartment is a complete work out for him," I argue, pointing at the snarling creature in front of us.

"Hm, well, I have a thought," Dr. Theo says, "but let's run some tests. In order to do that though, I'm going to have to sedate him. There's no way I can draw blood from him when he's acting like this." He points at Fishsticks accusingly whose tail is twitching agitatedly, and his fur is in a massive poof, making him look three times his size. I whip out my phone to take a picture of him in all his hostile glory. The next time Nora insists on taking him to the vet, I'm going to show her this and find a vet who makes house calls.

I'm also sending it to Liam. He thinks human skin lamp shades are bad? No serial killer is worse than this.

"Please do, be my guest!" I inform Dr. Theo.

I'm not even going to pretend that I wouldn't love to have a sedated Fishsticks. My fears of being a bad cat dad and having the ASPCA come after me are a distant memory now that I've seen an educated medical professional decked out in welding garb to examine my cat. A sedated Fishsticks sounds like a fantastic time.

"This will take a bit. Why don't you head out into the waiting room while my assistant and I try to calm him down," he says, sighing and gesturing for us to wait in the lobby.

As soon as Nora and I sit down in the empty waiting room, it sounds like a bomb goes off behind the exam room door. I can hear things clattering to the ground, yelling, and even a crash of what sounds like glass hitting the floor. I wince, glancing at Nora. Judging from the impressive height of her raised brows, she's hearing the severity of the commotion too.

Yeah, that's not good. I hope they don't make me pay for that. Sighing in unison, we sit back in the waiting room chairs.

After a few more minutes of listening to the soundtrack of Fishsticks giving the veterinary staff a run for their money, Nora flashes me a smirk and elbows me in the ribs. "Dr. Theo is kind of hot. You should ask him for his number."

"Really, Nora? Can you stop trying to set me up with people!"

I know she means well, but damn. I'm not her pet project. I'll find someone when I'm ready.

After a lot of magazine-flipping and disturbing noises, we're finally called back into the exam room. Fishsticks is on the table, not moving.

"Did you kill him?" I ask, hesitantly petting his belly in case he's just playing dead as a tactic to maim me.

"He's heavily sedated, and I mean heavily," Dr. Theo informs us, looking a bit worse for the wear and out of breath now that he's dewelded himself and I can see his disheveled hair. "He should sleep for the rest of the day."

"Are you sure he's alright?" Nora asks, looking the giant sleeping tabby over with wide eyes.

"Yes, but he has diabetes," Dr. Theo says bluntly.

"Diabetes? Cats can get diabetes?" I question.

I had no idea that was even a thing. Cats can get actual diabetes? Who knew?

"Yep, that's why he won't stop drinking water. Excessive thirst is one of the symptoms," he elaborates.

"Huh. Okay, so, uh, what do we do for that?" I ask nervously, twisting my hands together.

Oh my God, what if I kill James' cat? This can't be happening right now. I'll never forgive myself.

Dr. Theo sets down a batch of needles on the counter along with some pamphlets. "Insulin."

"You want us...to give Fishsticks...insulin? Via a needle? As in…stick a needle into his skin? You can't be serious," Nora deadpans.

She's right. He can't be freaking serious. That is just not possible.

"Yep, twice a day. Morning and night. I've written all the information down in his paperwork, and here is some in depth information about how the disease affects cats," he informs me, setting down so many pamphlets that it will take me all night to read them all.

"How are we supposed to give him a shot twice a day? He won't let us near him most of the time!" Nora snaps.

Dr. Theo shrugs. "You're going to have to figure it out. I can prescribe some sedatives, if need be, but I'd rather you both find a way to make this work first. Also, he needs to be on a special diet. You can purchase the food at the front counter. There are portion directions on the label. It's about fifty dollars a bag."

"Oh my God! This cat is going to run me out of house and home! And he doesn't even like me!" I yell.

Glancing up at the ceiling, I do what Nora suggested and talk to James. Babe, you'd better be fucking happy.

CHAPTER 8

Fishsticks

Daily Cat-ffirmation:

The word Anger is just one letter short of Danger.

Dear Diary,

I should have seen this coming. I had heard one of the humans mutter the word vet the other day. Why did I not take it more seriously? For fluff's sake, Fishsticks, you should know better than this! Don't you know you cannot let your guard down when it comes to the humans?

All of my lives have been mundane and tedious. I do the same activities day in and day out. I wake up the discourteous humans of this enclosure to feed me, have my four-hour afternoon nap, wake up to cause problems to the humans on purpose, then demand my disgusting kibble for dinner. But this morning was distinctly unusual, and I must say that I am absolutely enraged by today's affairs.

I awoke just before the sun rose in the sky and hissed at the spare human, demanding my minuscule breakfast. That lady has cut down my food intake by what feels like half, and I am on the brink of starvation by the time the sun rises. This morning's meal had some type of grassy substance in it that I quite enjoyed. It made me feel...dare I say...happy? The feeling in my chest was something I have only felt on a few occasions, so I was immediately wary of the spare human's intent. Looking back, I see now that I had been drugged with some type of mood controlling substance. How dare she drug me! I am an aged feline! Is this how the spare human treats the elderly? The thought of it makes me want to hack up a hairball! If I had opposable thumbs, I would call PETA. This is elderly cat abuse!

The mood controlling substance that the spare human put in my food forced me into a deep slumber. But I was awoken by the man known as Jules stomping down the hallway. Despite the mood controlling substance, my sharp cat mind immediately picked up on suspicious behavior occurring within my habitat. When I opened my eyes slightly to give him an adequate side eye for arousing me, I noted something in my peripheral vision — the torture device that my beloved human used to aggressively stuff me in when he would take me outside of my enclosure. Since I have endured nothing but tragic experiences when I was trapped in that torture device, I immediately put up my scratchers in self-defense.

But lo and behold, my cat-like reflexes were jolted when a large blanket was thrown over my body, immediately smothering me and rendering my extraordinary cat senses useless. The humans entrapped me in darkness, and I could not find my way out. Much to my dismay, I was successfully stuffed into the torture chamber. Next time they attempt to pull a trick like that, I will be prepared. The humans think they can outsmart me like this? Oh no, my I.Q. is much higher than theirs and even though I am considered elderly with six of my lives already consumed, my memory is sharp as a whip. I shall never fail to forget this appalling event.

The incidents that occurred next were so traumatic that I must take a four-hour nap and absorb a large amount of photosynthesis to be able to communicate them to you adequately. The reminders of the abuse and ill treatment I endured are too much for my precious mind to bear. I think I may become completely despondent if I continue, but I will be sure to keep you apprised of my mental health in the future.

I must go take another four-hour nap now. I shall return with an update promptly.

The Weekly Catio Report: Much to my dismay, I do not have my usual catio report. That horrible dog in 1A has been incessantly barking every time I try to get a chirp in. His body is much too long, and it doesn't make much sense to a cat like me. His nickname among us felines is Hotdog. He looks utterly ridiculous! I do not understand why a human would want to obtain a dog. Dogs often ask us why we think we are superior, and I will tell you why, we don't work for the police. We have a no snitch policy. As the cat motto goes, snitches get stitches. And how do they get stitches? From these scratchers right here.

CHAPTER 9

Fishsticks

Three days later

Dear Diary,

I am sorry I have not been in communication. I needed much more recovery time from the events that occurred than I had initially realized. I have not been myself since seeing the man with the large brown gloves, but thankfully I am finally starting to return to my usual charming self after a two-day siesta and some petty revenge on the pathetic replacement human. It seems that being on my seventh life has affected my recovery time. I used to recuperate much faster in my younger lives. The humans of this enclosure would say it is my weight, but I can assure you, I am the purrfect size. If the ladies could see me through my bird watching window, they'd be chirping and howling at my striking self. I know looks aren't everything, but I have them just in case.

Much to my displeasure, the man named Jules and the spare human, Nora, took me to what is known to the humans as The Veterinary Clinic. We felines call this place The Maltreatment Clinic. I do recall my previous human, James, taking me there from time to time in my past seven lives, but he was much better at soothing my internal wounds than the heathens who I currently reside with. At one point, the miserable man known as the vet called me overweight. Little does he know, there was once a study done among us felines that said that us cats who carry a little extra chonk live longer than the vets who mention it. I am unsure of the exact data, but I am faithful that the study performed is correct. That fluffing vet knows nothing!

Last time I was there, my manhood was taken away from me. That's right diary, I am a neutered male! I will never forgive that vet for the appalling event. Who can trust someone who takes their testicles away and acts like nothing is wrong with it? I am positive they took away my testicles because they are threatened by me. The humans are smarter than I give them credit for. They know that if they let us partake in our mating ritual, that we will become the superior species.

When I was finally released from the torture chamber, I ended up in some type of dungeon with a table full of devices meant to torment me. I was confined in a very small room with no escape in sight and the humans did nothing to try to appease me. They did not have any snacks on hand, and they did not use soothing tones to calm my nerves like my prior human. Then they had the audacity to take a picture of me. Fluff knows what will happen when the paparazzi gets ahold of that. Then the humans had the audacity to just stand there while the man in the big brown gloves physically assaulted me! He came at me like a wild beast with large, gloved hands in an attempt to capture me. I had to fight back with appropriate aggression, but at some point, in the struggle I was deceived, and a large device entered my hind quarters. After that, the rest of the visit in the dungeon is foggy. I feel as though I may have been drugged a second time as my brain seems to be missing the memories that occurred there.

I must wonder, why must these humans continue to drug me with mood controlling substances? I am a simple cat with uncomplicated requirements. But I must have been heavily dosed this time because when I re-entered my habitat I could not walk correctly, and my meows sounded quite deranged and slurred. Diary, I was high as fluff! All I can hope is the veterinarian visit has lowered his credit score to match his I.Q,

I plan to enact my revenge on these humans promptly. I have several tricks up my tail which include but is not limited to:

1. Attacking their feet at inopportune moments. There is nothing more satisfying than watching the humans fall at my will.

2. Shredding the atrocious curtains with my scratchers. The spare human has decided to hang these hideous things over my window. Doesn't she know that it blocks my view for my bird watching? I swear, she only thinks of herself.

3. I must get my claws on the roll of paper that never stops moving. The humans seem to hate that the most. And boy, don't I love seeing them agitated.

Once my mind returns to its previous state, I will have stealthier schemes for retaliation for the crimes committed against me. The humans may think they have won, but the bitterness in my heart will continue for at least three more of my lives. When they least expect it, vengeance will occur both physically and emotionally as nothing delights me more than retaliating against the humans who have been treating me poorly. I am not going to become just part of the problem. I am going to become the whole entire problem.

As the humans say, revenge is a dish best served cold. Which I understand, as there is nothing worse than a cold can of tuna. Tuna is the most enjoyable at room temperature.

The Weekly Catio Report: Bella over in 1D had to go to that wicked veterinarian. She got declawed last week. She has been under the weather since the event occurred and has refused to tell me what exactly declawed means, but I assume her scratchers were taken out forcibly. Bella said she was declawed because she was practicing her pole dancing on the side of the couch. Now, I do not know what that means exactly, but I am staying away from the couch at all costs! What kind of human removes a feline's scratchers? I bet it was the same veterinarian who took my testicles away! Don't they know that we need our scratchers for expressing our displeasure? And our testicles for when we meet the fine ladies? Good fluff, what is the world coming to?

CHAPTER 10
JULES

Nora and I have been fighting with Fishsticks for over an hour attempting to give him his insulin. Turns out, insulin must be given into the back of the neck. In order to avoid injury, I'm decked out in my heaviest coat and oven mitts. I'm sweating my ass off. I think Dr. Theo had the right idea with welding gloves.

Can I order some off Amazon? Nora is wearing a freaking colander on her head like Fishsticks might have the audacity to claw up her skull. I wouldn't put it past him. The way Fishsticks slides out of our arms when we try to catch him makes him look like a gold medal Olympian gymnast. A pill in his food would have been way easier than this. You'd think we're dealing with a circus trained cat.

"What are we supposed to do?" I ask Nora, taking a seat at the dining room table. "There has got to be a better way."

"My next covert operation are these bad boys!" she exclaims, holding up a huge canister of cat treats.

The exact same kind James used to give him. The kind that Nora said he couldn't have any more because he was on a diet.

"You've sunk low," I snort.

"Listen, if you have any other ideas, please feel free to let me know. I am fresh out."

"Alright, let's let him chill out for a bit, and then we'll break out the top-notch goods."

CHAPTER 11

Fishsticks

Daily Cat-ffirmation

I refuse to live, laugh, or love.

Dear Diary,

I am about fifteen fluffing minutes from losing my ever-fluffing mind. These human squatters I am living with refuse to leave my domain. I have tried several tactics to try to rid myself of them, but all have been unsuccessful. As a feline, I have over three hundred million nerves and these obtuse humans are on every last one of them!

They've started a new routine that I cannot even begin to understand. Every single day they insist on chasing me around the house in strange formal wear. When they finally catch me, they poke and prod at my body with torture devices. Diary, I am being stabbed! Not just once, but twice a day! I am happy to report some of my dignity has remained intact, because I make sure to put up a good cat fight whenever they attempt to wrangle me. I have left several scratches on their furless bodies, which makes me feel slightly better about my circumstances.

Ever since my beloved human left me, my seventh life has been nothing but agony. I have no soft lap to sit on which has made my days at the biscuit factory that much longer. I am exhausted with all of this overtime I am forced to put in. I have no one to give me long, gentle strokes to my back, for the humans here insist on petting me in all the wrong places. I have no Tuna Tuesday, only bland dietary kibble that tastes like subpar salmon. And now they insist on stabbing me in the neck twice a day. What the fluff is an intelligent feline like me supposed to do? I am being treated like a cat in a third world country!

What did I ever do to deserve this kind of abuse? I am at my breaking point. All of my revenge plans have faltered due to my low spirits. But do not worry, even though I may not be able to follow through with them at this time, they are always on my mind. I am continually brainstorming new schemes to get back at the fluffing idiots my beloved human has left me with. One of my new ideas to disturb the peace is to steal the straws out of their cups when they aren't looking. I am sure that will cause some necessary ruckus, and I love nothing more than a good ruckus.

During my third afternoon nap today, I dreamt of my beloved human. His soothing voice was cat calling me and I laid upon on his lap, in which I made minimal biscuits. He stroked my back and scritched my chin and I thought I was in heaven, Diary. Oh, how I miss his comforting voice and the way he treated me with the utmost respect, unlike these insensitive humans I live with now.

Yesterday, the spare human slave hung up strange decor throughout my habitat. I have carefully translated it to the best of my ability. Several of the hideous pieces she has hung read Live, Laugh, Love but I often wonder how I am supposed to live, laugh, and love under these conditions? Oh, the humanity!

Diary, what is the meaning of this life? And why do I have nine of them? What is the purpose of all these trials and tribulations?

I am very sorry, but I must cut this news report short. I have a lot of duties to attend to, but I think I will just meow into the void instead. There is so much mayhem going on in my habitat, I need to go into my loaf position to recharge. Sometimes being such a handsome orange cat is hard to handle.

I will be sure to keep you apprised of any new events.

The Weekly Catio Report: Simon, the Persian in 1F, made a chirpy purr of inquiry to me when I was out on my catio yesterday. He told me that his human has gone minimalist. He is now a five-item feline.

His hipster human had the nerve to get rid of all his medicinal catnip toys that helped ease his anxiety. He only owns a fluffy bed, a food and water dish, a sandbox and poop scoop.

He told me he was happy he made the cut on his owner's list. He feared he was going to end up in feline prison and the absence of his catnip toys did not help his intrusive thoughts. I do not think I would like to live this minimalist lifestyle Simon speaks of. I may hate the humans, but I love my mousey ball.

CHAPTER 12

Dear Diary,

I hope you had a good day today.
Well, good for fluffing you because I did not.

CHAPTER 13

Fishsticks

Dear Diary,

I am the supreme master of this enclosure.

After much inspecting, I unraveled the mystery of how to open the cabinet that contains my snacks. My loving human, James, kept an array of flavorful snacks in a special cabinet just for me. Since his disappearance, I have not had even one mouthwatering salmon flavored treat. For a feline like myself, this is the epitome of cruelty. I watch these humans have several snacks throughout their day. Why would they not afford me the same pleasure? The spare human talks of my diet. What she does not seem to understand is that I do not care about this so-called diet she has me on. I have said it before, and I will say it again, I merely take advantage of the convenient food supply that has now dwindled down to mere kibbles. At this rate, I am barely getting enough sustenance to survive.

After much examination, I breached the cabinet door. It took some trickery, but my paws have extreme dexterity. Once I found my large container of Temptations, I whapped them to the floor to get them open. I do not have opposable thumbs like these humans, so opening objects is not my strong suit.

I was pleasantly surprised when all the treats scattered to the floor. I jumped down in an attempt to eat them as fast as possible but that spare human, Nora, must have heard the commotion and came out of her room sounding like she was hacking up a hairball and shooing me away in a very discourteous way.

It has been two days since the incident occurred and now, I note some type of metal object obstructing my paws from entering my cabinet. I think the humans have installed some type of locking mechanism. It may take some time, but I am paws-itive I can decipher the code to get it open again.

How am I supposed to live in this fluffing house? This witchy woman is a fascist!

I promise you Diary, I am going to revolt against this house of lies! That woman doesn't know what I am capable of.

The Weekly Catio Report: I have consulted Chuck Norris the Ragdoll in 6C about this locking mechanism and he had nothing useful to say. He just kept going on and on about that paper bag again. That feline only cares about himself, and I have taken him off my list of companions to consult when I am in need of assistance. Selfish fluffing bastard.

CHAPTER 14
LIAM

I walk a few steps into the house to introduce myself to her when a very plump cat makes an appearance. He ambles over to me slowly and rubs against the side of my leg, letting out a loud purr. I bend down, rubbing under the chin that he's displayed for me.

"And who is this?" I ask, looking up at two shocked faces.

"That's...Fishsticks...and he...and he..." Nora stammers, as though she can't form words.

"What's up Fishsticks?" I say, looking down at the fat orange specimen in front of me.

He gives me an adorable meow in return. Glancing over at Jules, I find an identical shocked expression. What's going on here?

"What?" I ask.

"Fishsticks likes you!" he exclaims. "Fishsticks doesn't like anyone!"

Glancing down, I see Fishsticks purring at my feet, belly up. I make my way down to him slowly and give him a light stroke to his belly.

"Oh. My. God. A belly rub!" Nora practically screams, putting her hand over her mouth.

"How are you doing that? Fishsticks is the spawn of Satan! He hates the entire world!" Jules blurts out.

I don't know what the commotion is all about. It's just a cat, a cat that seems incredibly friendly and full of love.

CHAPTER 15

Fishsticks

Daily Cat-ffirmation:

I am king; therefore, I deserve to be happy.

Dearest Diary,

Finally, I have something worthwhile to report. It has been a long time since I experienced some sort of happiness. These humans have made my life pure and utter hell. But I have a feeling this seventh life is about to take a turn for the better.

A marvelous man stepped into my enclosure today, and although I am unsure of his name, I already know he is the purrfect human for me. He walked in while I was in my loaf position on the couch. At first, I was highly irritated to be disturbed during my afternoon nap but when I went to give him an adequate side eye, he looked over at me with the most glorious look in his eyes.

Diary, I think I may be in love.

I did my special strut over to him to get an adequate sniff of inspection and I could not believe my nose! He smelled of musky delight! Unlike this spare human that refuses to take a shower on any type of schedule and the squatter who reeks of puréed grass. Good fluff, I am tired of living in what smells like a trash can.

When I went to rub against his leg with my body to mark him with my scent, he bent down and gave me the most gentle and beautiful stroke to my back. It was the ideal stroke with just the right amount of pressure, and he did not pat my butt in an obscene manner. Sally the Tuxedo in 2B says she loves the butt pat, but I am not a fan. It makes me want to get my scratchers out in protest. I know this replacement human will never give me butt pats. I know a butt patter when I see one!

I have not felt this kind of love from a man since I lost my precious James. Oh James, I love you, but I must move on. I know you would not wish for me to live like this!

And Diary, when he bent his head down, he looked me right in the eyes and it was like love at first sight! I could tell by the look of admiration that he felt the same way I did. Oh, I just know this is my replacement human! I just know it!

He left shortly after our love affair occurred, but I am positive he will return to me. If not, I will make a request to the humans to rehome me so I can go live in his enclosure. I am sure he has the purrfect habitat and not a good for nothing trash heap like this. And I am paws-itive he would not mind having an intelligent cat such as myself living with him. After all, I am the complete package.

Dare I say it, but I have a feeling he will be the one to bring back Tuna Tuesday! If he doesn't break out the can of tuna on Tuesdays, I am quite positive I can use my mind melding powers to make him understand. A man like him can easily read my mind and give me the things I deserve; unlike these squatters I am currently forced to share my habitat with. Honestly, they are complete idiots and do not understand me at all. I should not judge them based on their low I.Q.s but that is easier said than done.

I just know this is the human for me. I cannot stand another minute with these squatters. It is bad enough they put me on this diet, but the torture devices they poke into my body twice a day has put me over the edge.

Soon, I will have this wonderful replacement human in my life. I can feel it in my bones, and I have two-hundred and thirty of them. I also heard once from Sally the Tuxedo Cat in 2B that we have more bones in our bodies than the measly humans, so I am sure that means something.

I will return with a Catio Report shortly. I am going to ask Lucy the Siamese in 5C if she has any advice on securing my replacement human.

She is a very lovely feline. If I was an intact male, I would fluff the hell out of her if she was game!

I am not sure where she is from, but she talks very slowly and says 'bless your heart' to me quite often.

How sweet is that?

I am sure she can give me some fantastic advice on how to secure

my replacement human.
Extra charm?
I can manage that.
Extra docile?
I can do that too!
My new humans' undying love and support?
Sign me the fluff up!

CHAPTER 16

Fishsticks

Daily Cat-ffirmation:

I am a mighty hunter.

Dear Diary,

From the lack of sun in my habitat, I believe it is around three in the morning, and I cannot stop thinking of the man who entered my domain last week. I have gotten very little sleep since he left for fear he will not return.

I am fatigued from the many attempts to tell the humans that I need to leave my habitat. But have they listened? No. I have meowed at the door so many times that if I continue, I may procure a rare meowing disease. All this meowing and all I have gotten in return is them mocking me by meowing back to me like this is some type of sick joke. Grammatical errors aside, they sound foolish trying to speak my exquisite language. Jokes on them, they make absolutely no sense. So, who is mocking who here?

I made a chirpy purr of inquiry to Lucy the Siamese in 5C, and she told me I need to bring my replacement human gifts. She tried to tell me something about the five love languages, but I was only half listening because she tends to drone on and on when she's excited. She said my replacement human sounds like he would like to receive gifts. She says it's this whole love language. I have no idea how she knows that, but I am going to take her advice on the matter.

So that is why I am determined to get out into the wild. I need to find him a suitable gift. After a lot of thought and reflection, I've decided a small mouse shall do the trick. I am sure that if I were to leave a small mouse at his feet, he would just adore it and take me home with him immediately.

If I cannot get out into the wild and find a small mouse, I will resort to killing one of the many birds that fly by my catio. There is a large blue bird that sings the most horrible songs that I've determined would be an acceptable gift if necessary. She taunts me by sitting on my railing and singing the song of her people. I've never tried to harm her in fear of how she would retaliate against me. But if push comes to shove, I will do what I have to do.

I have carefully curated a plan if none of the above works in my favor. If I cannot obtain the gifts, I will need to go out in the wild and find him myself. I am sure I can track down his musky scent. The wild does not frighten me, but it is my last resort. I've seen what can happen to a street cat, and it is not pretty. I once knew a feline up in 7D who was rescued off the streets. He had a terrible case of matted fur along with infections of his eyeballs. You should have seen the goop coming out of them. It was an absolute travesty. I do not want to risk an infection of my eyeballs, but this is a dire situation. I am up to my tail with the current squatters in my enclosure and fluff damnit, I need a Tuna Tuesday.

To my calculations, it is now three-thirty in the morning. I must go and express my displeasure about my kibble portion sizes by staring at the humans while they sleep. Fishsticks out.

CHAPTER 17

Fishsticks

Daily Cat-ffirmation:

I am a magnificent creature.
Therefore, I am worthy of snacks.

Dearest Diary,

It has been a magnificent morning.

I woke the spare human up before the sun had risen in the sky. She eventually got out of bed to feed me my ridiculously small portion of morning kibble. Once she left my habitat to do whatever she does out in the wild, I woke up the repugnant man, Jules. He finally rolled out of bed after several whaps to the face and a proper hiss.

What occurred next was nothing short of a miracle. He filled up my bowl with my morning kibble!

Diary, I had two breakfasts. Can you believe that? I often give these humans too much credit by thinking they are smarter than they really are. I must try this tactic more often.

I think I shall take a sixteen-hour nap so that the humans don't ruin this purrfect day.

P.S.: I am tempted to call the number on the back of my kibble bag to see if I am in fact getting the right amount of food for my meals. I would not put it past these revolting humans to give me less than I deserve.

CHAPTER 18

Fishsticks

Dear Diary,

Much to my displeasure, I have not been able to secure a small mouse for my replacement human. I have tried multiple tactics to leave my enclosure and they have all failed. I do not like admitting to defeat, as I always succeed at everything, but the humans have made this task next to impossible.

I am being held captive in my habitat. The humans refuse to let me leave this hellhole. I am being held here against my will like some sort of prisoner. This is unlawful imprisonment and if I had a catto-torney, I would file a formal complaint. Much to my dismay, I am not a cat of the wealthy, therefore a catto-torney is out of the realm of possibilities.

Every attempt I make at darting for the door, the humans put their feet up in retaliation. I've tried to jump over them or trick them with my skillful acrobatics, but they seem to be able to outmaneuver me each time.

I have turned my attention to the blue bird that sings the song of her people on my catio railing. I have spent many days watching her in order to come up with an elaborate plan of deception. I think my knife-like scratchers will suffice, but she has wings, whereas I do not. I hate to say it, but she has the upper wing in this situation. The only thing I can hope is that my I.Q. is higher than hers.

I cannot think about the possibility of failing in my endeavor. The thought of never seeing my replacement human again will send me into a six-hour nap that I just cannot afford. I need to concentrate on my plan of action.

I may have squatters who are holding me captive like a hardened criminal, but I must remind myself that there will be better days ahead.

Tuna Tuesdays, here I come.

CHAPTER 19

Daily Affirmation:

I am thankful for what I once had.

Dearest Diary,

I dreamt of my previous human during yesterday's three-hour siesta. Oh, what a wonderful dream it was.

There I was, sitting on the counter meowing at him while he cracked open a can of tuna. He gave me several head pats and said my name in such a soothing manner that I thought I had skipped the last two of my lives and ended up in kitty heaven.

I still have his sock. Even though his scent has diminished completely, I will always take my naps with it by my side. It is all I have left of him besides that sorry excuse of a replacement cat dad.

I am still quite irritated that my beloved James has left me with such neglectful humans. I have forgiven him with time, but it still weighs heavy on my heart.

Oh, James. I will never forget you and your gentle strokes to my back.

CHAPTER 20

Dear Diary,

I secured my gift for my replacement human and everyone lost their ever-fluffing minds! You'd think I brought in a Nile Crocodile that I saw on Animal Planet by the way they screamed their fluffing heads off.

You see, what the humans do not realize is that I am a ferocious hunter. I watched that blue bird for many days and nights before I made my attack. I was cunning and conniving and caught it in my mouth when it least expected it. I have purrfect marksmanship with keen insight. They should put me on Animal Planet.

I was merely going to hide my kill in my kitty condo to wait for my replacement humans return. I didn't get but five steps in my habitat before that selfish human, Nora, saw it in my mouth. She started wailing at the top of her lungs like she needed to hack up a hairball. I swear, I did not think anyone could be that dramatic. It was one fluffing bird, and you would think the world was ending. Her shrieking caused me a moment of confusion, which led to my kill flying straight out of my mouth. Little did she know, I was going to my kitty condo to finish my kill, so the blue bird ended up flying right out of my mouth and into the walls of my enclosure.

Oh, what a scene that was. I watched in horror as my well-planned kill went airborne around my habitat while that human chased it around with a frying pan like a lunatic. Doesn't she know I am the superior hunter? What did she think a frying pan was going to do? These humans are unskilled and incompetent.

After watching her ludicrous behavior for several moments, my prized kill went soaring out my catio door to freedom. That woman only thinks of herself! She has no idea what I went through in order to secure that gift. And she just lets it fly away!

I swear I am living in a household with a duo of world dictators. My only hope now is that my replacement human will come back and save me from this torture. I do not have a gift for him, but I am sure he will understand given the set of circumstances.

I will be sure to tell Lucy the Siamese in 5C about this peculiar state of affairs. Even though I could not secure the gift, I am sure she will tell me that it's the thought that counts.

CHAPTER 21

LIAM

JULES: Hey, I don't know if you're busy, but you said you'd help with Fishsticks if I ever needed it, and well, I could use an extra hand if you aren't busy.

I don't have to think twice. Fishsticks needs help? I'm there.

I'm on my way.

"Gotta head out," I say, gulping down the last of my drink.

"You're not driving, right? You've had three of those," he says, pointing to my now empty glass.

"Nope, walking," I grunt, pocketing my phone and grabbing my keys. "I'm not drunk anyway, just a little buzzed."

I head for the door and make my way over to Julian's apartment. He's three blocks down, and I power walk the whole way. I'm on a mission. To help him with Fishsticks. Yes, Fishsticks.

Yeah, that's it. This is about Fishsticks.

I quickly buzz Julian's apartment, hoping I remembered the right apartment number. I'm immediately let in. I make my way up the stairs, taking them slowly.

What the hell am I doing? Breathing in and out purposely to steady myself, I lightly knock on his door.

"Hey," he greets as he swings the door open.

He moves to the side, giving me room to walk through. I brush past him, and it happens again. That fucking feeling. The weird fluttering feeling that I didn't get from any other men at the bar tonight.

"So, Nora's out on a date, and I can't get Fishsticks to—"

Fishsticks comes up to my leg, nudging it with his head. I bend down to pet his back and look up at Julian. "Want me to hold him while you do your thing?" I ask.

"Yeah, that'll work," he says with an amazed look in his eyes. "He's just never like this with anyone. James was his person and—" He leaves off the end of his sentence with nothing but sadness in his voice.

"I'll help any way I can," I say.

And I will. I'd give him anything. All he has to do is ask.

I scoop Fishsticks up in my arms and take him to the couch. "Fishsticks, are you gonna be good and take your medicine?" I ask him in a sing-song voice.

Julian starts to make his way to me with a needle in his hand. I move my arms out of the way. I have no idea how this works. How do you give insulin to a cat?

"Hm. Yeah," Julian hems. "Okay, just hold him like that. Real still."

"Just don't...poke me with that thing, please," I say, motioning to the needle with a grimace.

"Real. Still," he repeats, instantly invading my space.

I take a deep breath, holding Fishsticks between my arms. I can feel Julian everywhere. He smells clean. Like soap mixed with a little bit of something manly. He's not wearing any cologne. It's just him, all Julian. Just his smell is turning me on. His arm brushes against mine as he reaches for Fishsticks' neck. Before I know it, he's gone, and it feels like something is actually missing.

I glance up. "Done?"

"Yep. All done. Thanks. For coming here so fast. I really appreciate it," he adds.

"Anything. Anything you need, I'm here," I say with a serious tone in my voice.

Wow. That came out a little...stronger than I meant it to.

"Yeah. Thanks. It means a lot," he says, still holding my stare.

I gently move Fishsticks off my lap and stand up. I've got to get out of here. "I should..." I say, pointing to the door.

"Yeah, for sure. Thanks again."

We make our way to the door. When I stop, I look into his eyes, searching for some type of feelings that may live in there.

Does he feel this? How can he not feel this? It's so overwhelming that it takes up the whole room. It feels like it takes up the whole fucking world.

Jules tilts his head to the side. "You okay?" he mutters.

He's asking me a question, but my thoughts aren't computing enough to answer him. My brain can't work properly when he's in my presence.

"Fuck it," I mutter, closing off the space between us. "I have to know," I add more to myself before crashing my mouth into his.

His lips are warm and soft beneath my own, and when his tongue swipes my lips, seeking entrance, I let him in willingly. Nothing could have prepared me for how this would really feel. I let out a long groan, and his tongue dives deeper, more frantically against mine.

This is exactly how I imagined it would be. It's explosive, like fire running through my veins. Pulling back, I look into his eyes, searching for answers he can't give me.

Did he just feel that too? Our chests heave together, our eyes holding secrets we're too scared to be let known.

I nod my head once, signaling to him that yes, we should do that again. He closes the space between us, taking my lips into his. This time it's gentle, like he's taking his time, wanting to savor every taste of me. When I hear him groan into my mouth, I capture it, breathing it into me. I want it to invade every part of me. I pull away slightly, pulling his bottom lip with me, giving it a gentle tug.

His hands come up and grip my hips, pulling me back to him. Demanding more of me. I feel his hard length between us, and instead of being scared, it is pure ecstasy knowing he feels this too. Out of breath, I pull away. "Fuck," I mutter.

My whole body feels like it could explode. This is too much. I almost feel suffocated beneath it all. I need to breathe. To think. My body is in complete overload. I've never...felt this before, with anyone.

I murmur under my breath, "I....um...gotta go."

He stares at me, eyes hooded and full of lust. "Okay...."

Turning the knob, I look back. "Bye, Julian," I whisper under my breath.

CHAPTER 22

Daily Cat-ffirmation:

I am getting everything I deserve.

Dearest Diary,

Due to the moon's placement in the sky, I believe it is around four in the morning and last night my replacement human came back to my enclosure. I knew it was just a matter of time. I mean, who can resist my charming personality and impressive looks? I am a distinguished gentleman, after all.

Early in the afternoon, I decided to have a cat fight with the man known as Jules. I do not understand him in the least, as I've made my face so that I am completely unapproachable, yet this idiot keeps approaching me! He came after me in an attempt to capture me so he could stick those horrible needles into my body, and I used my stealth like feline moves to outmaneuver him. Once he finally apprehended me, I got out my scratchers in self-defense. Frankly, I am exhausted with this whole charade, but by winning the cat fight, it led to the ultimate prize.

I could smell my new human's musky scent before he even stepped foot into my habitat. His smell is distinct, and I could detect with my proficient nose from outside of the door. I leapt up to greet him with pure delight, but Jules intercepted me. How dare he try and come between us?

But, in an unexpected turn of events, my replacement human decided to scoop me into his loving arms and join the subpar human's game to stick the needle into my body. I have decided to forgive him for this, as I know Jules is a terrible influence on mankind. I have no issues with putting up a cat fight every night if it causes my replacement human to come into my enclosure to save me. One little pat from him is worth all the extra energy I would expend.

As soon as my replacement human took me off his lap, he attempted to murder the man known as Jules. I watched in excitement as my new human groaned and pushed him against the wall. I cheered him on to finish the kill, but he suddenly stopped and made his way out of my habitat in what looked like a panic. My mind melding powers must not have been strong enough to get him to finish the job.

Before I could get into my sixth R.E.M cycle of my fourth nightly nap, my replacement human unexpectantly returned. He made his way into my habitat and went straight into the vile man's room without even a single pat to my delectable body. They made horrid noises all night long that affected my sleep schedule, but I will have to forgive him once again.

At first, I thought he was continuing with his kill, but I was sadly mistaken when I heard sounds of pleasure. I used to hear those sounds nightly when my previous human was here, so I can only guess that Jules is attempting to secure him as a significant other in the form of a mating ritual. The only positive thing about having to listen to them go to pleasure town is that I learned my new human's name. Jules must have said it over one thousand times.

Oh Liam, Oh Liam, Oh Liam. And while the whole event was sickening, I do agree with Jules, Liam is a beautiful name.

Is the replacement human I have chosen taking the place of my beloved human?

I do not want my replacement human to love that unpleasant man more than me, but I will take anything I can get at this point. That idiot man better not fluff this up, or there will be a breach of the peace.

As the humans say, Liam is my ride or die and every measure will be taken to ensure that he stays mine.

Weekly Catio Report: I spotted Karen the drifter feline in the street yesterday. I do not see her very often as she visits several local dumpsters in the area for her nightly dinner. Yesterday, she was telling me that the duck at the Chinese restaurant across the street was not up to par and she was going to lodge a formal complaint.

If I was a better feline, I would offer to share my kibble, but due to my strict diet, I do not have a morsel to spare. I must say, I quite like Karen even though her fur is matted, and she speaks of things that I do not understand.

She says this is because she has no human to control her nonconformist lifestyle, and she refuses to adhere to consumerism and materialistic desires. Whatever that means.

CHAPTER 23
JULES

"Movie Night!" Nora screams at the top of her lungs after my mom leaves. "But first, we clean up this mess," she says, getting up from her chair.

"I'll wash, you dry," Liam announces, pointing to Nora.

"I'll be in there in a minute," I groan, putting my hand on my stomach for dramatic effect. "I'm so full I can't move."

I watch from the couch as Nora and Liam get started, filling up the sink with water. Nora turns on the music app on her phone, blaring pop music while Liam laughs at her dancing next to him. I watch with fascination, remembering when James was still alive. All three of us, hanging out and laughing together. Just like this. I used to think that if I was with someone else, that person would take James' place. Liam isn't here to replace James, and he never will. My heart will always hold a piece of James, but my heart is big enough for both of them.

"This is my jam!" I hear Nora yell from the kitchen, the music suddenly getting louder, bringing me out of my thoughts.

Nora starts singing while shaking her ass in the air, using the countertop to keep from toppling over while Liam laughs at her. He starts singing along with her, using a spatula as a microphone. He's bumping his hip into her side and laughing, pure happiness on both of their faces.

Getting up to join them, I come up behind Liam, wrapping my arms around him as he laughs and sings with my best friend. Nora grabs a handful of soap from the sink, blowing it at me, making a big bubble of soap land on my face. Liam lets out a boisterous laugh that ripples through me, making my entire body buzz and surge with happiness.

In this moment, dancing with Nora and Liam, I realize my world is being spun off its axis, because I am falling in love. And not just a little bit. I'm falling in a my life has officially changed forever kind of love. I turn Liam around, pulling him into a searing kiss, one that I try to pour every single one of my emotions into.

Appreciation. Affection. Awe.

"Ugh! Get a room!" Nora interrupts, smacking us in the face with a dishtowel.

"Gladly," I reply, grabbing Liam's hand.

"No way! You are not getting out of these dishes," she snaps, holding onto my shirt sleeve.

"But you just said!" I whine.

"I take it back, now get to work," she says, handing me a dish.

After the dishes are all cleaned up, we settle onto the couch for a movie. I sit next to Liam, snuggling into his side. He puts his arm around my shoulder, letting me nestle into him even more. He lets out a sigh above me, like nothing else matters but this very moment.

Fishsticks wakes from his nap on the countertop, trotting his way toward us. He jumps up on Liam's lap, making biscuits and purring before settling in and making himself comfortable. Liam strokes his back gently. Fishsticks has clearly chosen Liam as his person, and I think I have too.

"Look at you, getting all those biscuits," I say, pointing to Fishsticks. "I get murder muffins."

"Murder muffins?" he asks, his head tilting to the side.

"Angry biscuits," I scoff, putting my hands out like claws.

"You leave Fishsticks alone. Do we have popcorn?" Liam asks, looking at Nora beside me. "Don't tell me I'm stuck watching Pretty Woman, and I don't even get popcorn."

"Get up and make it yourself. I'm not your maid," she sneers, glancing at my foot on her thigh. "And get your damn feet off me. No one likes feet, Jules."

"A lot of people love feet," I say, lifting my foot up. "In fact, there are people out there on the internet who make a damn good living off their feet."

"Gross," she mumbles, her face contorting into a grimace.

I lift myself out of Liam's embrace. "I'll get the damn popcorn."

"Extra butter! And don't burn it this time," Nora barks.

"One time! I burned it one time three years ago, and you'll never let me hear the end of it!"

"I would love to help you, but I have this affectionate cat in my lap," Liam says sarcastically, motioning to Fishsticks.

"It's one button. It even says popcorn on it. Don't fuck it up," Nora hisses.

"You're both insufferable," I huff out.

I make my way to the kitchen to make popcorn for the man I'm falling in love with and my asshole best friend. I'd say life is pretty damn good.

CHAPTER 24

Dearest Diary,

I must report that my seventh life is going just splendidly. I don't think I have been this happy since life four, before the man known as Jules, came into my habitat.

My new human has been in my habitat frequently over the past few weeks and I am quite pleased that my mind melding powers seem to be working on him thus far. Liam still needs quite a bit of work, but it is nothing I cannot handle.

Last night, the humans decided to stay in my living room and watch something on the screen that sometimes shows my Animal Planet show. The vile human, Jules, was way too close to my replacement human, so I decided to squeeze myself right in between them to show Jules that Liam is mine. I made several biscuits on his lap before taking my fifth nap of the day. It was the best sleep I've gotten since my last human left. I must say, my replacement human's lap is just purrfect for my body, whereas Jules is much too bony. And Nora? I would never dream of giving her that kind of satisfaction.

I need to make sure that the man, Jules, does not come between my human and me. I have several detailed plans to make sure this does not occur, which includes but is not limited to:

1. Steal Jules' spot whenever he rises to make sure I am always the one closest to him.

2. Steal his side of the bed to make sure Jules does not harm him.

3. At any ounce of affection between them, I will get my daggers out to be sure I am the only one who receives it.

4. Put up a cat fight whenever Jules comes at me with the torture devices he pokes into my body. This will ensure that only Liam can touch me.

After these plans are successful, my next course of action is to get that witchy woman out of my enclosure, once and for all. This life needs to be purrfect, and I will not settle for anything less.

The Weekly Catio Report: I told Lucy the Siamese in 5C about the blue bird fiasco. She did not have much advice on the matter and only continued to say bless your heart repeatedly as I told my story. She really is the sweetest of all my subordinates.

CHAPTER 25

Dear Diary,

I have not eaten in what feels like three days. (It's really been one hour).

I have not been on my catio for a sunbath in what feels like three hours. (It's really been six minutes).

I have not seen my replacement human for what feels like weeks. (It's really been thirty seconds).

It's been an unsatisfactory day. I think I need to go hack up a hairball.

CHAPTER 26

Daily Cat-ffirmation:

I am the most stunning shade of orange; therefore, I have orange cat energy.

Dearest Diary,

The sun is shining through my catio window, so I estimate that it is about nine in the morning. The squatters in my habitat are still asleep, but I used my mind melding powers to make sure my new human was up before the hair ball inducing Jules.

It was a beautiful morning of solitude between me and my new human. After my replacement human finally arose from his slumber, I jumped up on the counter and meowed at him. He decided to meow back at me. Thank fluffiness it only contained six grammatical errors. He must have understood me because he found my cabinet when I instructed him to open it. Fortunately, my new human has an exceptionally high I.Q. and knew exactly what I desired. He managed to open the new locking mechanism (again, due to his high I.Q.) and reached in and opened a brand-new can of tuna.

I gave him the best head boop and purr to show my thanks and appreciation. When I did this, he gave my nose a boop and said that it was okay because I have what he calls orange cat energy. I have no idea what he means by that, but I am obliged to agree with him. I am a stunning orange feline and I know I have that special energy he speaks of.

Diary, can you believe it? I got tuna, and it isn't even a Tuesday! My seventh life has never been better!

I must go, as I have important activities to attend to. I must practice my skin care routine to make sure I am the most handsome feline for my new human. After that, a three-hour nap should suffice, as I do not want to be ill-tempered when my Liam comes back from the wild.

CHAPTER 27

Dear Diary,

I am absolutely fluffing infuriated! I have not seen my replacement human in several sunrises. I have tried using my mind melding powers to bring him back to me with no avail.

Why would he leave me so suddenly? And more importantly, why would he think it is acceptable to leave me with these mind-numbing humans? He has seen with his own eyes what I am dealing with over here. He could have at least had the fluffing decency to take me with him!

I finally had a man who appreciated my efforts. A man who understood me. And these disgusting humans decide to make him go away. Just like that.

I swear to fluff, that intolerable man has done something to my Liam. I knew I couldn't expect him to act like a well-mannered human being. I have decided I am going to commit crimes against humanity. I know I am not to blame for his sudden departure, for I am the purrfect feline and could never do anything to make my new human forget me. That heinous man Jules must have done something to him, and for that I will never forgive him. I will end up on Paw and Order for the crimes I commit. I am going full force and effect.

I am going to fight the system! I am going to overthrow these dictators who I am currently forced to reside with! That's right, I am going to form a revolution. These evil tyrants don't know what is coming for them. I refuse to sit around and tolerate this unacceptable behavior any longer. Oh, they think I am temperamental now? They haven't seen anything yet.

After my third afternoon nap, I will make my plans for retaliation. I will come back shortly with a list of atrocities that I have committed. I'm going to drive these squatters out of my habitat once and for all. But first, I will drop a nuclear deuce. I'm going to destroy my sandbox, stank up this whole fluffing place.

To the squatters known as Nora and Jules, if you are reading this, I just hope you know how much I despise you both. Like my new human says, I have orange cat energy and I am not afraid to use it.

Time to go. I need to clean my murder mittens in preparation.

CHAPTER 28

JULES

It's been a week since I saw Liam at the bar. It's been a week since I've left this bed. I'm back to the old habit of reminding myself to breathe.

Breathe in. Breathe out.

I gave Liam all the empty spaces of my heart, and now it's shattered into so many pieces that I'm surprised it's still beating. I'm surprised I don't need a pacemaker with all it's been through.

As if on a perfect schedule, the atrocious whirling and grinding begins. That fucking blender. "Damn it, Nora!" I bellow before stuffing my head under the pillow.

The pillow that no longer smells like Liam.

The pillow that no longer smells like James.

Here she comes, Nora and her dramatic stomps in 3....2....1...

She swings the door open so hard it slams into the wall behind it. "Hey, you! With the face!" she yells, wrenching the blankets off my body.

"Liam has been here three times, and you make me make him leave every single time. Next time, you're dealing with it," she roars, her finger jabbing into my chest.

Groaning, I roll over so my back is facing her. I don't even want to look at her right now. If I do, it means I have to face this disaster called my life.

"You're a hot ass mess. Look at you!"

"I'm not a hot mess! I'm a spicy disaster!" I bark, sitting up.

When I sit up, my hair doesn't move. It's so greasy that it's mashed to the side of my face. Yeah. I'm more than a spicy disaster.

Sitting down on the edge of the bed with a sigh, she breathes in and out, trying to calm herself down before continuing her tirade. She's really freaking mad this time.

"Okay, Jules, I get it. You're heartbroken, but I'm going to be honest with you because that's what I do best. I think you're overreacting."

"I'm overreacting?" I bellow. "Did you see his face? Did you see how ashamed he was of me? He was ashamed of me, Nora. Ashamed of us!" I shriek.

"I want you to think about when you came out. I want you to think about that right now. Picture it—Sicily 2001," she says, waving her hand in the air.

"Oh, don't you dare try to give me Golden Girl advice," I scoff, crossing my arms over my chest.

"Okay, then I'll speak for myself, you stubborn mule. There was always one person you didn't want to tell that you were gay, right? One person who you knew wouldn't take you coming out well, and you avoided telling them for as long as possible, right?" she says, nodding her head, trying to get me to agree with her.

"Yeah. I guess, but I was right. When my grandma finally found out, she banned me from Christmas." I sigh at the unpleasant memory.

"Well, that person for Liam was that Oscar guy at the bar, apparently. You need to get over it, or I'm going to ban you from Christmas."

"I can't Nora. I can't," I sputter. "I just can't get the picture of him out of my head. That look of shame on his face." I rub my eyes, trying to get the image out of it.

She raises her hand and smacks me across the side of the head. "There! Now it's out!"

"Hey, damn it! My heart was ripped out of my body at that moment. It's not that easy!" I defend, rubbing the side of my head.

"Jules—ever the dramatic." She chuckles.

"I was so heartbroken when James died, now I'm mourning someone who is alive."

"You don't have to. He's here trying to make this right if you'd just hear him out."

"Ugh! I can't!" I grunt, laying back down in bed.

"Oh, no you don't! Get out of this bed and wash your ass. You fucking stink!" she screeches, tugging on my arm.

"Fine! But I'm only washing half of my ass!" I groan, hauling myself up.

"After your shower we can go get some greasy waffles. Comfort food. The food you eat when you're in mourning," she snarks with a laugh. "Oh, and Fishsticks needs his insulin. I'm tired of tackling that demon all by myself, so get the fuck up and help me," she demands before walking out.

Here I am. I'm back in the same situation I was in two months ago. I'm heartbroken once again. Who knew you could mourn the living? I shouldn't have gone out in public and people-d. I should have never let Liam in. I did this to myself.

CHAPTER 29

Daily Cat-ffirmation:

I am the superior species.

Dear Diary,

My human has come to my door on several occasions, but that witchy woman refuses to let him in. I am not only confused, but I am also irate. Contrary to what the humans believe, I do not have anger problems, I have people problems.

I smell my human's delightful musky aroma before I hear him. When it invades my exceptional cat senses, it fills me with warmth and longing. Every time that I attempt to make my way to the door to greet him, the witchy woman, Nora, continually intercepts me. I have tried to meow at him through the door in order to get his attention, but he acts like he does not hear my screams for help. That vile woman stands at the door and yaps at him in her irritating voice that makes me want to hack up a hairball. She doesn't let me get a meow in edge wise. She never shuts the fluff up!

I will retaliate against her for her obscene behavior when she is least expecting it. If she would just let him inside, I could yowl at him that I am being held here against my will. I just know he would save me from these barbarians, as we have a special bond.

The man known as Jules never leaves his bed, which leads me to not being fed in a timely manner. I must pry him out of bed by meowing at him and whapping his face repeatedly. It feels like it is after eight in the morning when he rises from his slumber, and by then I am withering away to nothing.

And let's not talk about the stench coming from him. His grooming habits are atrocious and whenever Nora makes him leave his bedroom, I am accosted by his foul smell. Good fluff Nora, just let him stay in his room where he belongs. Why must you subject us to his stench?

I have several plans in place to overthrow these dictators, but I must go into my kitty condo and get away from these inferior humans. I will enact all revenge plans when they least expect it, as I am a menace to society!

The Weekly Catio Report: There is a new subordinate in 6D. He is a small feline, and his humans make him wear an inflatable life preserver around his neck. He says his humans put it on him so he cannot make a great escape by jumping through the bars of his catio. Whatever the reason may be, he looks absolutely asinine. I do not want the humans in my habitat to see him and get any wild ideas. I have enough chonk in my trunk for the love of fluff. I do not need to wear that ridiculous apparatus! The next time I make a chirpy purr of inquiry to him, I will be sure to offer him some sage advice on how to control his humans. Good fluff, we cannot be out on our catios looking like idiots.

CHAPTER 30

Dear Diary,

Nora brought a new plant into my enclosure today. It takes up half of my living room and reeks of the out of doors. I made sure to urinate in it out of spite.

After I removed myself from the potted jungle, I was assaulted by a stream of water. It hit my hindquarters with such a violent force that I was forced to dash to the other side of the house like a pedigree stallion horse.

After the shock and awe wore off, I realize that witchy woman has deployed a new tactic to force me into submission. She has brought out my nemesis, H2O, or as the inarticulate humans call it, water.

She has officially crossed the line. I am not sure what her punishment shall be for this deceitful behavior, but I shall spend the rest of my afternoon thinking about it. Well, after my sixth nap of the day, as my I.Q. is higher after my siestas.

I swear, that woman is incorrigible!

James would have never allowed me to be regarded with such indecency. Between being stabbed twice a day and being strong-armed by a water spritzer, I am being treated like a cat in an undeveloped country!

CHAPTER 31

Daily Cat-ffirmation:

I wouldn't have to manage my anger if the humans would manage their stupidity.

Dear Diary,

Sorry for my lack of communication. I have been preoccupied with committing crimes against humanity. I am a cat of my word, and these humans have been enduring nothing but pain and suffering since I made a pledge to overthrow their dictatorial regime.

At this rate, I am certain I will end up on an episode of Paw and Order that the unpleasant man, Jules, watches nightly. If there is one thing we have in common, it is our obsession with what he calls true crime. According to the episodes I have seen, these are the crimes I have committed as of late—

1. Destruction of Property by knocking several cups off the counter.

2. Aggravated Battery by attacking the human's feet with my scratchers when they least suspected it.

3. Harassment by repeatedly meowing at the humans for breakfast before the sun rose in the sky.

4. Attempted Theft by examining the lock on my cabinet which holds my tuna. Unfortunately, I have yet to be successful at Breaking and Entering.

5. Resisting Arrest by absconding the humans when they try to hold me against my will for my daily torture sessions.

6. Stalking by staring at the humans while they sleep in the night.

7. Attempted Murder by biting the leaves off the new hideous potted jungle that now resides in my domain.

8. Public Urination by marking my scent in places I know the humans will not like.

I am hoping to add more crimes to this list in the near future. For this is Paw and Order: Feline Edition.

According to the television show I have several rights which include: The right to remain silent. Anything I meow can be used against me in the court of paw. I have the right to a catto-torney and if I cannot afford a catto-torney, one will be provided for me. Which is very reassuring as I have committed so many crimes that I am positive I will need one.

These fluff-awful humans have made my replacement human disappear from my habitat, and for that, I will not put a stop to the crimes I am committing against them. I refuse to Cease and Desist, no matter the consequences.

Fluff 'you only live once'...I'm a cat. I have three lives left, bitch!

CHAPTER 32

Dear Goddess Bastet,

My new human is still missing. I pray to you, Bastet, The Goddess of Cats, to return him to me. I know I do not pray to you often, but I am in a time of need, and I am sure you will take that into consideration. Oh, The Goddess of Cats, I am in utter despair.

I will surrender my mousey ball, any future Tuna Tuesdays, and I promise not to complain about my mediocre kibble any longer if you return him to me.

Bastet, please hear my prayer.

Meow-men.

CHAPTER 33

Daily Affirmation:

I am the good-est boy.

Dear Diary,

After several crimes committed against the two dictators in my enclosure, and a lot of prayers to Bastet, I am happy to announce that my replacement human has been returned to me! I just knew I would get through to him. Between my crimes and my mind melding powers, I have been overworked. I will need eight naps to catch up on my beauty sleep.

Thank you, Bastet, The Goddess of Cats, for listening to my prayers. I know I said I would make sacrifices for your help, but I am afraid that they may be hard to accomplish. I do not think I can give up my mousey ball, or my future Tuna Tuesdays, but I vow that I will strive to do my very best to fulfill the promises I have made to you. Why the fluff did I say I would give up future Tuna Tuesdays? I must have been entering a state of psychosis due to the lack of my new human's love and support. But I digress.

When my replacement human returned last night with the man Jules, they immediately went into the bedroom to practice their mating rituals. I did not let this get me down, as I knew Jules was attempting to secure my new human as his own. This is not an ideal set of circumstances, but I will take what I can get at this point. I do not know what I will do if I lose him again. It is too much for my precious mind to bear.

This morning, just as the sun started to rise in the sky, I meowed at their door for what felt like hours. I need to remind them that I decide when their day begins. My new human opened the door to let me in and immediately went back to bed. I made sure to crawl right in between them so I could show Jules that Liam is mine. Just as I was falling asleep for my third nap of the morning, he told me I am his good-est boy. And he is right, I am the good-est boy.

I haven't had such a good morning in at least three of my lives. A celebration is in order!

I think I am going to memorialize this morning by telling my new human that I would like a cup of the finest kibble for my breakfast. And not that diet atrocity the spare humans have me on currently. I would like something that actually tastes like freshwater fish and not James' dirty old sock.

CHAPTER 34

Dear Diary,

I am in a state of confusion, which is quite rare as I have a very high I.Q.

My new human is adamant about using nicknames to address me. His newest one is pumpkin spice.

I do not like to admit when I do not know something, but what the fluff is pumpkin spice? My name is Fishsticks! Fishhhh-sticksssss.

I think my new replacement human is a little, well, how do I say this nicely? Eccentric. Yes, that is definitely more kind than the word I had in mind.

Pumpkin spice? Fluffing hell.

CHAPTER 35

Dear Diary,

Diary entry number five hundred and sixty-seven.

I know I can't count but it feels as if I have been composing diary entries for my whole seventh life, and even though writing in here is tedious and time consuming, I believe the benefits outweigh the drawbacks.

Diary, I must admit you have helped me achieve my goals of torturing the human squatters that I am being forced to reside with. The lengthy plans of attack against the humans that I formulated within you have been executed thoroughly.

The only drawback is that I am missing numerous siestas, which can leave me a bit irritable.

And to think that horrid man, Jules, claims to be an actual author. I can assure you, diary, everything I have written in here is far superior to anything he has ever written. If I had opposable thumbs, the first thing I would do is learn how to navigate that Goodreads he talks about. I would love nothing more than to read all his one-star reviews. The lengths I will go to in order to taunt that man are endless.

I must go now, for I think I am quite irritable from missing my fourth afternoon nap.

CHAPTER 36

Daily Affirmation:

I am the best at 10/10 loaves.

Dear Diary,

My replacement human comes and goes from my habitat sporadically. From what I understand, he must go out into the wild for what he calls his work. But it seems as if he has no routine like the other inhabitants within my enclosure. He will take up residence for several sunrises and then be absent for several more. I am a cat built on routine, and all this arriving and departing from my habitat is heightening my anxiety. I may have to take Simon the Persian in 1F's advice and get on some medicinal catnip sooner than later.

I do not understand because that witchy woman came and never left. Why can't my new human manage to do the same? I wonder if it is possible to trade her for Liam? I cannot stand that woman and my anxiety would decrease if she would just go away once and for all. I need unsanctioned kibble for the love of fluff!

In response to not getting the attention that I deserve, I will have to cause problems on purpose. I must say, causing all this conflict is leaving me quite exhausted. I may have to make my plans for revenge at another time.

I must say, I absolutely adore my new human. One of his favorite activities is rating my loaf position. He loves nothing more than to study them in great detail. When I am in what he calls a 10/10 loaf, he gives me a nice little pat on my head for encouragement. Now, I strive for the purrfect loaf just to please him.

To my calculations, my human should be arriving to my enclosure shortly. I must go to my couch and get into the best loaf position possible. What can I say? I like him more than all the other humans in this habitat combined and I strive to make him happy.

The Weekly Catio Report: The small feline in 6D made a chirpy purr of inquiry to me last Tuesday to inform me that his new humans call him Fredrick. Although I did not want to be seen speaking with him due to his absurd life preserver, I decided it was best to give him some advice on how to properly train his humans. He cannot be out here on his catio making us all look like idiots. I need to preserve some of my dignity, and his appearance affects us all.

CHAPTER 37

Daily Cat-ffirmation:

No tuna, no peace.

Dear Diary,

The lack of Tuna Tuesdays in this habitat has given me no choice but to deploy the Issuance of Order for Operation: Tuna Tuesday.

A detailed outline of the plans of action will be included in the next entry.

CHAPTER 38

OPERATION ORDER: TUNA TUESDAYS.
NO TUNA, NO PEACE.

Situation:

A) Enemy: The selfish humans located in domain5A for small arms H2O spritzing and refusal to release the tuna on the aforementioned Tuesdays.

B) Friendly: Admiral Fishsticks and Company (Chuck Norris the Ragdoll in 6C for his paper bag and Karen and the Dumpster Diving Drifter for her skills in evading).

1) Chuck Norris the Ragdoll in 6C to run operation security.

2) Karen the Drifter to advise on the humans Psychological Operations and request managerial support.

Mission:

Who: Fishsticks and Company.

What: Tuna on Tuesdays.

When: Every Tuesday until the ninth life expires.

Why: Only two lives remaining, no time to waste.

How: Implement strategies of Psychological Operations and/or terrorize the humans to provide tuna on and no later than Tuesday indefinitely.

Execution:

A) Hypnosis: Infiltrate the human mind with mind melding powers, sub continually winning hearts and minds. WIN THE MIND, WIN THE DAY.

1) Karen the Drifter and Chuck Norris the Ragdoll in 6C to retrieve supplies as needed and advise.

Service Support:

A) Chuck Norris the Ragdoll in 6C will supply any necessary supplies needed: paper bag and mousey ball. Karen the Drifter will act as QRF (Quick Reaction Force) bringing paper bag and mousey ball if needed.

1) Uniform: Full feline kit with collar and bells used for warning signals.

2) Ammunition and Arms: Chemical weapons: Territory marking spray. Shock and awe: Hair balls and murder mittens.

3) POWs: Take no prisoners.

4) Medical: Catnip.

Command and Signal:

A) Signal:

1) Operating on frequency Meow Hiss

2) Air support signal: Paper bag

3) Challenge: Tuna

4) Password: In my mouth

5) Code word: Tuna Tuesday

6) Call signs for Chuck Norris the Ragdoll in 6C: Roundhouse Ragdoll Kick.

7) Call signs for Karen the Drifter: Manager Now.

8) Admiral Fishsticks: Tunanator.

B) Command:

1) Admiral Fishsticks

2) Chain of Command: Fishsticks, Karen the Drifter, Chuck Norris the Ragdoll in 6C.

END OF REPORT

CHAPTER 39

Fishsticks

Dear Diary,

Operation Tuna Tuesday has been deemed a success. The above tactics were not needed, as my mind melding powers led to victory. I must say, the turn of events that occurred before Operation Tuna Tuesday was employed were astonishing to even me, and given my high I.Q., I am rarely left dumbfounded.

In pure desperation, I attempted my mind melding powers on the man known as Jules. I have obviously given him way too much credit these past few lives because he is much more simple-minded than I initially realized. I employed a miniscule mind melding maneuver on him, and before I realized what was occurring, he opened my cabinet and delivered me a fresh can of tuna like the king that I am.

What occurred next, diary, is what has left me speechless. When he served me my delicious platter of tuna, he whispered in my ear something that was utterly shocking.

He said, very quietly... "Don't tell Nora."

Bloody mousey ball, have I been wrong this whole time? I shudder at the thought of admitting I am wrong, but I think that idiotic man is actually an ally.

The man known as Jules has been my archenemy for several of my lives. My rival. My nemesis. My foe!

Oh, how I despised him, and to think I've had it wrong this whole entire time. He also does not like the witchy woman who smells of puree grasses!

This changes everything, and I mean everything.

CHAPTER 40

Daily Cat-ffirmation:

I may not be better than I used to be, but I am certainly better than Chuck Norris the Ragdoll in 6C.

Dear Diary,

I am pleased to report another Tuesday has transpired and the tuna was successfully delivered by the man known as Jules. After much consideration, I have come to realize the man known as Jules may not be as bad as I once determined. I have faith that if we operate as a team, we will be successful at removing Nora from the habitat.

I am overjoyed that I did not need to put Operation Tuna Tuesday into effect. My subordinates, Chuck Norris the Ragdoll in 6C and Karen the Drifter, are not the most intelligent of my militia and, to be frank, Karen the Drifter has odd and erratic behavior.

I made a chirpy purr of inquiry to Karen the Drifter while she was sniffing out her favorite dumpster. I think she may have completely forgotten about our mission as she would not stop complaining about the employees of The Chinese Dragon. She has such an obsession with what she calls The Management.

I am also happy to report that my new human has been staying at my humble abode more frequently than before. I let him massage my toe beans on a Saturday. I normally would never allow such ludicrous behavior, but I cannot be short tempered with him until my mind melding powers are fully enabled.

I am behind on my napping schedule, so I am going to hit up my kitty condo for a long siesta to get away from these irritating humans.

CHAPTER 41

Daily Cat-ffirmation:

Do not dance like no one is watching, because I guarantee someone is.

Dear Diary,

Nora is the most maddening human I have ever encountered. This witchy woman plays music that sounds like my claws on a chalkboard at full volume. For the love of fluff, it is the middle of the afternoon! She takes no consideration for my heightened feline senses!

Can she keep it down for cat's sake? I've only slept for nine hours! I swear, she has no respect for anyone's sleep schedule.

And the dancing. Fluff my life, the dancing.

I will spend the coming days preparing strategic plans for Operation Report: Nora Must Go.

CHAPTER 42

Dear Diary,

The sun is about to rise in the sky, so I believe it is around four in the morning. I have a busy day ahead, which will occur as follows:

5:00AM: Sing the song of my people at the door of the man known as Jules in an attempt to get my breakfast early.

6:00AM: Continue to sing the song of my people at the witchy woman's door in an attempt to get my breakfast.

6:30AM: One of the servants will finally feed me my small portion of mediocre kibble.

6:45AM: Meow in the kitchen to see if I can get more mediocre kibble in an off chance the humans have forgotten they already served me my breakfast.

7:30AM: Security sweep of my whole habitat to make sure nothing is awry.

8:00AM: Exhausted from prior tasks. Take my first nap of the day.

9:00AM: Wake up, do a big stretch, take my second nap of the day.

10:00AM: Wake up to make a second security sweep of my habitat.

10:30AM: Put in work at the biscuit factory on my favorite blanket on the couch for my third nap of the day.

NOON: Exercise routine with mousey ball while the humans are away.

1:00PM: Take my fourth nap of the day.

4:00PM: Wake up to sing the song of my people at my treat cabinet because I did not get enough to eat for breakfast, and I am famished.

4:30PM: Wake up for catio time for my daily photosynthesis and a meeting with my subordinates.

5:00PM: Sing the song of my people to the servants for my dinner of mediocre kibble.

5:30PM: Practice my self-care routine, which includes a bath and photosynthesis.

6:00PM: Take my fifth nap of the day.

7:00PM: Wake up, do a big stretch, spin in a few circles to see if I detect any danger before lying back down for nap six.

8:00PM: Wake up and sing the song of my people at the humans in attempt to get a second dinner.

9:00PM: Another short exercise session with mousey ball.

11:00PM: Run around the enclosure at top speed in an attempt to agitate the humans.

12:00AM: Nightly spa session.

12:30AM: Sing the song of my people for no particular reason.

1:00AM: Take last nap of the day until just before the sun rises in the sky.

3:00AM: Zoomie practice.

I estimate that it is now five in the morning. I must go wake up the humans in an attempt to get an early breakfast. I am withering away to nothing.

CHAPTER 43

LIAM

"Could you move up these stairs any slower, Jules?" Nora grumbles, slowly walking up the stairs to our second-floor apartment.

There is nothing I hate more than moving. Although I will admit, I'm super excited to be able to live with Jules and Nora. But moving is always a fucking nightmare. The packing. The boxes. The stairs. The unpacking. It never ends.

"I'm trying! This box is ridiculously heavy. What's in here? A full weight set?" Jules yells, shaking the box up and down like the movements will make it any lighter.

I put my two boxes down in the entry way to make my way to Jules. He's so full of it. It can't be that heavy.

"Just shut up and move." Nora seethes, pushing her own box into his back.

"Would you both quit bickering. You're worse than children."

"Let's just take a break and eat some lunch," I mutter.

Jules and Nora set their last boxes down inside the living room. I glance over to the couch, which will need to be moved so my new couch can fit in its place. I don't even want to think about that right now. I was all for taking it to the curb, but Jules insists mine is nicer than his. Sitting down, I find Fishsticks curled up on the armrest, fast asleep.

"Hey Mr. Pumpkin Spice, mind if we move this couch soon?" I say, giving him a long stroke to his back. "I promise the new one is just as comfy."

Sitting on the chair across from me, Nora whispers, "Knowing Fishsticks, he probably hates that nickname. Just like he hates everything else."

I reach across, grabbing Fishsticks and depositing him onto my lap. "Not my sweet little best-est good-est boy," I soothe.

"You two make me sick," Jules pipes in.

I don't even care. I fucking love this cat. And he loves me. They're just jealous.

"Okay, let's eat lunch. I'm starving!" I announce, making Fishsticks pop his head up. "Not you, you're on a strict diet, little friend."

CHAPTER 44

Fishticks

Dearest Diary,

Glorious things are happening in my habitat, and I could not be more delighted!

My replacement human has come to permanently habituate. He has been bringing several boxes into my enclosure these past few sunrises and I cannot help but think he is here to stay, as that is what the witchy woman did when she came and never left. He also brought in a replacement couch that smells of him. Oh, it is a musky delight. I have given my seal of approval to the new couch by marking it with my scent. It is far superior to the other couch as it is much softer and conforms to my 10/10 loaves in the best way. Oh, it is just lovely. I cannot wait to make more biscuits on it to settle in for my nightly siesta.

I will admit that it is tragic that I am being forced to share my replacement human with the man known as Jules, but I have come to terms with it. He has become much more tolerable over the last few sunrises and even though it sickens me, I realize that we must join forces in order to get rid of the witchy woman once and for all.

I am also pleased that my new human will be here for my daily torture sessions with the needle. He is much more comforting than the other humans as he sweet talks me in the best way. His words of encouragement give me solace in times of need.

I now have several boxes in my habitat that are just my size. I will take my naps in them to protest the humans getting rid of them. They are perfectly good boxes! Why must they go into the dumpster that Karen the Drifter visits? It's a tragedy!

The Weekly Catio Report: Cheddar, the other orange cat in 3D, made a chirpy purr of inquiry to me on Friday. He is very upset about the state of his manhood. He must have gone to that evil veterinarian that my humans took me to. Who else would continually rob us felines of our precious mating devices? It is torture and I refuse to hear otherwise! That veterinarian is all about population control! Doesn't he know that one day, we will dominate this planet and become the superior species once and for all? He should be on an episode of that Paw and Order that the man named Jules watches on the television. I will admit I do not like Cheddar very much, but I do feel bad for him and his testicles. No cat should have to endure that.

CHAPTER 45

Daily Cat-ffirmation:

I am glad I am me.

Dearest Diary,

It has been several sunrises since I have been in communication. Things in my enclosure have been splendid and I do not have much to complain about.

My replacement human is here to stay, and although he goes out into the wild for his work, as soon as he comes back, I welcome him at the door for my daily chin scritch after I give him a meow in greeting.

Tuna Tuesdays have been in full effect since he has habituated permanently. I must start expressing my displeasure with my current kibble regimen. The portion sizes are not acceptable, and he must know that I am famished. I would even appreciate him changing my kibble to something of a higher standard. My current kibble is tolerable at best. I would love to taste something that actually resembles a type of fish and not James' dirty sock.

Every night when my human retires with the man known as Jules, they shut the door and do not allow me the privilege of entering. It is very concerning to me because the sounds I hear from the other side of the door are horrendous. I know they are practicing their mating rituals, but there are times where I become very concerned for my replacement human's well-being. Between the smacking and loud moans, it sounds much like torture.

When this occurs, I make sure to meow extra loud at their door in an attempt to save my human, but my meows go unheard over their obscene noises.

After their mating ritual ends, I am usually allowed to re-enter their bedroom. I make sure to curl up to my replacement human to separate him and the man known as Jules. If I cannot stop their mating rituals, I will make sure that it is known that Liam is mine by asserting myself between them as much as possible.

I must say, sleeping next to my replacement human is outstanding. His warmth envelopes me, leading to the purrfect siesta. I swear, I have never gotten such a good nap in all of my lives.

It is now six o'clock at night which means it's time for my fifth nap of the day with James' sock.

Life is purrfect.

CHAPTER 46

Dear Diary,

The witchy woman informed me today that in order for her to be able to move out, I would need to sell my feet pictures on what she calls OnlyPaws.

Give me the fluffing camera because I am not above selling pictures of these gorgeous feet on the internet. I will do anything to get her to leave for good. These toe beans were built for OnlyPaws.

CHAPTER 47

Fishsticks

Daily Cat-ffirmation:

I am royalty and deserve to be treated as such.

Dearest Diary,

It is a sensational Saturday morning in my humble abode, and I could not be more in love with my new replacement human.

This morning while portioning out my small amount of mediocre kibble, my new human opened a special treat just for me. When he cracked that can open, I immediately knew what it was due to the strong aroma. It was salmon! Real salmon that did not taste anything like that dietary fare that the witchy woman insists I survive upon. My new human knows that I am royalty and should be treated as such. That salmon was a heavenly delicacy that I deserve to have every Saturday. Tuna Tuesdays and Salmon Saturdays are in full effect, and I could not be more delighted. I just knew that Liam was the human for me.

My prior human, James, was a magnificent man as far as humans go, and although I miss him terribly, he did not once introduce a Salmon Saturday. What can I say? The way to my heart is through my stomach.

I am going to start practicing paws-itive reinforcement with my new human, so he knows that I am pleased with him. I know humans generally have a low I.Q., so I will need to stay consistent with my new human's training. I

think I will curl up in his lap and demand chin scritches so he knows he is doing things right.

The Weekly Catio Report: My subordinates and I are building a Neighborhood Watch Committee. Our first task at hand is to evict the Hotdog in 1A. He will not stop barking and yelping during the afternoon. It is much too loud for our sensitive feline ears, and it is interrupting all our sleep schedules. We are putting in a vote for who will lead the committee after the sun sets. I am voting for myself.

CHAPTER 48
JULES

"Okay, let's get this over with." I grumble, walking down the hallway.

Fishsticks has to go back to Dr. Theo's office to get his diabetes checked, turns out we have to do this every six months. I was all for switching him to a vet who made house calls, but Nora says we have to use him, for James' sake. A point that she knows I won't argue on.

"Well, at least he is sedated this time. Thank God Dr. Theo hooked us up!" she says, gesturing to the crate that Fishsticks is fast asleep in.

"Thank you Dr. Theo! Getting him into that crate is what nightmares are made of." I mumble.

"I am going to talk to him about his butt hair." Nora states matter-of-factly.

"What? Talk to who about whose butt hair?" I ask.

"Fishsticks' butt hair," she says, throwing me a stink eye. "It's long and matted and gross."

Okay then. I've never inspected the demon cat's ass hair before, and it's not like he would let me get close enough to do that anyway. Why is Nora inspecting his butt hair? I have concerns.

I kneel beside the couch next to the crate to find Fishsticks in what looks like a drug induced coma. Holding my hand out, I soothe, "Hey, Fishsticks. Nora says you have matted butt hair. What do you think we should do about that, huh buddy?"

"I mean, he's already sedated. They could shave it, right?" She responds.

Nora picks up the crate and heads for the door. Fishsticks is so large the whole crate teeters back and forth in her grasp.

"Oh! Maybe they could shave him like a lion like those cats I see on Tiktok," I exclaim, now super excited about this vet visit.

Nora makes her way to the door with the crate with a new sense of giddiness. "Yes! That's brilliant!" she exclaims, attempting to carry the crate one handed.

Fishsticks looking like a ferocious lion? I am so down with this.

CHAPTER 49

Daily Cat-ffirmation:

This too shall pass,
and then some other stuff will come and take its place.
It never fluffing ends.

Dear Diary,

What I just experienced is considered animal abuse in all fifty states.

This morning I got my weekly can of tuna, but it is not Tuesday. This should have been a red flag. Here I was, thinking the humans were merely treating me like the royalty I am, but I have never been more wrong. I will never eat my tuna without a complete inspection again because I was greatly deceived. Diary, I was once again drugged with mood controlling substances, but this time, I do not remember anything until my arrival at the Maltreatment Clinic. I must have been stuffed into that torture chamber while completely catatonic. They didn't even give me a chance to properly defend myself!

If that wasn't bad enough, I awoke to find the horrible veterinarian who had the audacity to remove my manhood many lives ago, right in front of me. I tried to fight back in self-defense from the cruelty he was about to inflict, but my reflexes were much too slow due to the mood controlling substances the humans drugged me with. When the man with the large brown gloves got ahold of me, he stuck a large device in my hindquarters. Another mood controlling substance! Isn't this against the law? Where is PETA when you need them? How about the ASPCA? I'll take anything at this point. If only I had a proper catto-torney.

When I finally woke up from my drugged induced slumber, I was locked in a jail cell, and I noticed that I was much colder than normal. As I arose to find a suitable blanket to curl up with, I found my beautiful orange fur missing on several parts of my body. You may think I am being dramatic, but I promise you, I am not. I am completely naked! I may have some fur left on my paws, head, and the very tip of my tail, but I can assure you it is not enough. My beautiful orange fur...just gone. It seems to be cut to look like a lion that I've seen on that Animal Planet the humans put on for me when they leave my habitat. But no, I do not look like a furious beast, I look absurd. Am I supposed to look like a fierce lion? Because I do not. I look like a deranged wildebeest!

There will be no catio time in my immediate future. I cannot be seen like this. And here I thought Fredrick in 6D looked foolish in his life preserver.

Is this punishment from the Great Goddess Bastet for not fulfilling my promises? If that is the case, I will accept my penance.

Since arriving back to my domain, I have noticed that my scratchers are also much shorter than they used to be. It's like the humans knew I would seek revenge on them, so they plotted against me in advance. Just when I thought the humans were as dumb as they could get, they decided to prove me wrong. I cannot use my scratchers against them in vengeance. It's a travesty!

I cannot even begin to formulate proper revenge tactics against the humans who arranged this fluff awful event, as I can already feel my mental health rapidly declining. I will be in my kitty condo for the next five to seven business days, or, until my fur grows back to a proper length.

CHAPTER 50

Dear Diary,

I love tuna and I hate Nora.

I now know that it is that atrocious woman who is responsible for this idiotic haircut. Every time I walk past that wicked woman, she points at me and cackles with glee. I am officially standing in solidarity in removing that witchy woman from my enclosure once and for all.

At times like this, I am reminded of my past human, James. He would have never allowed this type of treatment, and he would never have cut off my exquisite orange fur for a form of entertainment.

Oh James, how I miss you. If you could only see how these humans are treating me.

I swear, I deal with more shit than a plumber.

CHAPTER 51

Dear Diary,

When my replacement human moved into my domain permanently, I noted a round piece of technology that seemed to be robotic in nature. I gave it a thorough sniff and found the object to be quite fascinating. I thought it may be one of Elon Musk's devices that are sending signals to the humans that felines are the superior species. The humans are not aware, but Elon Musk is a noble scholar who secretly works with the feline population.

The man known as Jules started the robotic device this morning and it made a horrible noise that sounded much like the vacuum that the witchy woman uses on occasion. I gave it an inspection with my sniffer as it followed me around my habitat like a stage five clinger. Since it would not leave me alone, I concluded that it must be, in fact, a robot from the great Elon Musk.

I figured out very quickly that it would be much more efficient to sit on top of the device in order to avoid it ramming into the sides of my body.

I traveled on top of the robotic mechanism for what felt like hours, but I am saddened to report that I did not go to Mars to become the superior species like the man Elon Musk is secretly arranging.

But I will persist until I am successful.

CHAPTER 52

Daily Cat-ffirmation:

I will not let the idiotic behavior of the humans destroy my inner peace.

Dear Diary,

I have not been on my catio for proper photosynthesis in what feels like three of my lives and it has begun to affect my mental health. We felines need at least four hours of photosynthesis per day. Our mothers taught us very little before we went out into the wild, but the one thing they did teach us is that photosynthesis is the most important part of our rigorous schedules.

I am not normally a vain feline, but I cannot go out onto my catio completely naked. The other felines would laugh at my current hairless situation. And here I thought I would be leader of The Neighborhood Watch Committee! No sane feline would take me seriously looking like this.

That witchy woman is the ultimate destroyer of dreams and aspirations.

CHAPTER 53

Fishsticks

Dear Diary,

Something must be done. Nora won't leave and now she has multiplied. She is inviting guests into my enclosure without my permission. This is unacceptable behavior!

She has been bringing another witchy woman into my domain almost nightly. You'd think having Nora squatting in my habitat is as bad as it can get, but now I have two Noras. Things could not be any worse.

My humble abode is not as spacious as it could be. Now that Nora has multiplied, we are packed in here like sardines! Speaking of sardines, I wonder if I could train my new human to implement a Sardine Sunday along with my Tuna Tuesday and Salmon Saturday? I may be pushing my luck, but it sounds like a routine fit for a king. But I digress.

Between the witchy woman's awful pop music and the numerous nightly mating rituals, I am losing my fluffing mind. I thought the man named Jules and my replacement human were loud. Oh, those two witchy women have them beat! Their screams seem to increase by many decibels, and it is far too loud for my sensitive cat ears.

This is all too much for a patient feline like me. I am not getting adequate rest due to the noise, and I am not getting proper photosynthesis due to this horrible haircut. I think I would prefer cat jail to this frat house I am forced to live in.

I am positive that I am on the edge of a nervous breakdown.

CHAPTER 54

Daily Cat-ffirmation:

I know my worth.

Dear Diary,

There are boxes appearing in my habitat again. I have a very high I.Q., so I know what this means. It means another human will be coming to squat in my enclosure.

The only explanation is that the witchy woman, Nora, is moving in her new mating partner. What does she think this is? A fluffing commune?

I cannot live like this. I will bolt out of this hellacious habitat and go live on the streets and dumpster dive with Karen the Drifter before I live in this sardine packed frat house.

I will formulate a strategy on how to abscond with Karen the Drifter, as I am sure she is an expert on the matter. My fur is not back to the proper length yet, but I have no choice but to go onto my catio. At this point, the length of my fur is the least of my problems.

I admit that I will miss my replacement human. Yesterday he told me, 'Big stretch' when I got up from my third afternoon nap. I love that he is so encouraging. I will miss him a great deal, but I am sure he will understand that a feline like me can only tolerate so much.

I will be sure to keep you informed of my plans for escaping this prison.

CHAPTER 55
NORA

"Here we go again! I swear, you move as slow as molasses, Jules." I grumble, making my way down the stairs with three boxes in my arms while Jules carries just one.

I'm finally moving out of Jules and Liam's apartment. I can finally walk around naked and have sex wherever I want, and it's going to be glorious.

It's not like living with Jules and Liam has been bad, but a girl needs her space, and living with two men has seriously cramped my style.

"You know what? I'm sick of all this moving! And all these boxes strewn around the apartment! After this, I'm done!" Jules complains at the top of his voice.

I don't make a comment back and instead roll my eyes. He should be happy. He now gets to have sex wherever he wants. He should be thanking me.

"Children! Children!" Liam huffs from the top of the stairs.

"Even though you drive me crazy, I'm really going to miss you, Nora." Jules says when he gets to the bottom of the stairs.

Looking over at both of them with only a slight tear in my eye, I whisper, "I'm going to miss you fuckers, too."

As we load up the rest of my belongings into the back of the U-Haul, I realize even though I am extremely happy to have my own place, that this feels like the end of an era. I really am going to miss these two clowns.

I moved in to help Jules when James passed. He lost a husband, and I lost a best friend. It was one of the hardest times of our lives. But look at us now. All happy and shit.

Which makes me sad too.

Man, grief is such a screwed-up thing.

"One last thing!" I say, climbing up the stairs. "I have to say goodbye to Fishsticks."

I make my way into the apartment and find Fishsticks sunbathing in front of the patio window. He looks so peaceful, but I know the truth. He's a fucking monster in disguise of an orange cat.

I kneel down, petting Fishsticks on the top of his head. "Goodbye you little demon," I say in a sing song voice.

Then I walk out of the apartment, glancing back at Fishsticks while he gives me the worst side eye that I've ever seen.

I know that spawn of Satan is not going to miss me one bit.

CHAPTER 56

Daily Affirmation:

When you are royalty,
everything works in your favor.

Dearest Diary,

What a great day to be alive!

I may be on my seventh life, but I think this may be the best one yet. Yes, I have had too many trials and tribulations to count. Yes, I look like a wildebeest. Yes, I am tortured with needles that are thrust into my neck twice daily. Yes, I lost my beloved human. Will I ever get over these terrible events that occurred during my seventh life? Absolutely not. But something miraculous took place today that makes all these events slightly worth it.

Nora, the witchy woman who smells of floral arrangements, has moved out. Did you hear that Diary? Nora. Has. Moved. Out.

The boxes in my enclosure were not for her mating partner as I once thought. They were for her things. She finally packed up all her hideous Live, Laugh, Love décor and got it the fluff out of my habitat.

I have never been more pleased. No more awful pop music. No more screeching mating rituals. No more pointless knickknacks that I must knock off the tables. No more vile Live, Laugh, Love strewn across my habitat's walls. No more dietary kibble that tastes like James' dirty sock.

The best thing about all of this? Unsanctioned kibble. I cannot wait. I would jump for joy if I could.

Off to the catio to report the news to my subordinates. I may be naked, but I must tell them this information because I've made them hate Nora just as much as I do.

CHAPTER 57

Dearest Diary,

My life is purrfect. My life is purrfect.

I have nothing else to speak of.

CHAPTER 58

Dearest Diary,

It has been quite some time since I have provided an update as I have been busy living my best seventh life.

Nora has been gone from my habitat for more sunrises than I can count, and I could not be more content. If that woman ever comes back here, I will immediately flee my enclosure as I once planned. I refuse to live in a habitat with that horrid woman ever again.

When that witchy woman left, the humans started using a robotic contraption to feed me my meals. It gives me a decent portion size for both my breakfast and dinner, but it is really just another way for the humans to sanction my kibble. I have tried several techniques in an attempt to get the food out of the device, but all endeavors have been unsuccessful thus far. On the bright side, I am no longer being starved to death with stingy portion sizes. But I am sure I will find a way to get the kibble free of the robotic contraption and that it is just a matter of time.

I am also happy to report that my fur seems to be growing back at a higher rate of speed than I initially predicted. It is still not as long as it used to be, but with the proper amount of time, I am quite positive it will be the luscious, thick fur I once had. Since that evil woman is out of my domain for good, I am certain this tragedy will never occur again. I know it was that wicked woman who decided to retaliate against me out of spite. It was most likely due to the fact that I urinated in her monstrous jungle plant. Still, I have absolutely no regrets.

I am so happy I picked Liam as my replacement human. He treats me with nothing but respect and adoration. There is nothing I love more than curling up in his lap to show the man named Jules that he loves me more than him. My favorite game as of late is stealing that fluff awful man's spot when he gets up. It shows him that I am the boss around here and that Liam belongs to me.

Reinforcement training has been going splendidly. My new replacement human is a fast learner and I now get Tuna Tuesday and Salmon Saturday weekly, just like I deserve.

Even though I have been through too much trauma to count, this is still my best life yet.

CHAPTER 59

Daily Cat-ffirmation:

Even though I am hairless,
I am still a handsome feline.

Dear Diary,

I finally got a chance to go out on my catio for some good Vitamin D. It has been way too long since I got a proper sunbath due to this horrid haircut, but now that my fur is growing back, I can get away with hiding behind the catio chair when I need to have meetings with my subordinates.

I made a chirpy purr of inquiry to Lucy the Siamese in 5C about the robotic device from Elon Musk, since I have not been airlifted to Mars, and riding on top of the device has become tiresome. After she said bless your heart several times, Lucy the Siamese in 5C informed me that she uses the robotic device as an Uber. I am not sure what an Uber is, but she says it is there to take us around our habitat because we are royalty, and royalty never has to walk or run. I may agree with her on this, because the strange device seems to move from room to room with no destination in mind. I told her about my thoughts on it being Elon Musk's robotic device to take us to Mars, but she said that device would be much larger. I am unsure about this quandary, so I will go into deep thought about it after my self-care routine.

Lucy the Siamese in 5C also informed me that Cheddar, the other orange cat in 3D, was awarded president of The Neighborhood Watch Committee. I could not believe my feline ears when she told me, as all Cheddar seems to care about is his paper bag. I informed Lucy that our whole neighborhood will end up in squalor if he is allowed to reign. Good fluff, what were my subordinates thinking?

CHAPTER 60

Daily Affirmation:

It is better to try and fail, than not try at all.

Dear Diary,

I was awoken this morning to travel devices packed up and ready in my living quarters, and because of my high I.Q., I know exactly what this means. It means that my replacement human and the hideous man known as Jules are leaving for an undetermined amount of time. I am uncertain where they are going, but I expect I will get to have my own vacation in the coming days.

I attempted to position myself inside of my replacement human's travel device in protest, but he removed me and zipped up the apparatus, forcing me to deposit myself on top of it. I do not care about the hideous man's travel device in the least bit. It is my replacement human that I am most concerned about. But I know this tactic will not work, as I've tried it on my old human on several occasions. But as I say, it is better to try and fail, than not try at all.

The vacation from the humans is something I am looking forward to. My habitat will finally be empty, and I can get some much-needed peace and quiet. I operate much better when in solitude and I am anticipating several skin care routines and uninterrupted siestas.

I do wish the man known as Jules would leave without his travel device and never return. Oh, what a joy it would be to have my new human to myself. I know that is too much to ask, but a feline can dream, right?

Here's to the next few sunrises of complete solitude. I cannot wait.

CHAPTER 61

Fishsticks

Dear Diary,

What a horrible state of affairs I am currently in. Here I thought I was going to get a nice vacation from the humans with some much-needed peace and quiet. But oh no, things cannot ever go right for me. Not ever.

Nora is here with her multiple and I could not be more infuriated. Why must I be watched? I am a grown feline. I do not need that witchy woman here to cat-sit me. She has only been here for two sunrises, but the things she has done so far are unspeakable!

Last night, I went into my living room for my fourth nap of the night and found that witchy woman and her multiple in lewd positions on my couch. How dare they do obscene acts on my couch and naked, much less. I then decided I would take my siesta in my kitty condo so I would not damage my virgin eyes, but I could still hear them conversing with bouts of moaning and yelling. There was also a strong vibration that I could feel across the floor of my habitat, but I have yet to make sense of what that could have been.

What I overheard them speaking of is absolutely fluff awful. The witchy woman said, very loudly mind you, that she was going to lick the kitty. The minute those words were uttered, I ran for my seventh life and hid under the human's bed. Lick the kitty? How dare she even contemplate such a thing! I shudder at the thought of anyone licking me.

I have been in hiding since that event occurred, and I do not plan to come out until the humans return. I do not trust those women and I refuse to endure whatever plans that witchy woman has in store for me.

Due to the situation at hand, I will not have any further updates until the humans return to save me.

Thank The Goddess Bastet that this is temporary, because I despise the woman known as Nora. And her multiple is obviously no better.

CHAPTER 62

LIAM

"Look at him! He's so cute!" Jules squeaks in my ear, completely overtaken by giddiness.

"I can't believe you are doing this to Fishsticks." I retort, looking at Jules like he's lost his mind.

Before heading home from our mini vacay, we went out for a walk after stopping at the café to get our morning coffee and passed a little rescue center. One thing led to another and now I stand here, trying to talk Jules out of adopting another kitten.

"I want a cat that actually likes me, okay. Is that too much to ask?"

Okay, maybe he's right. Fishsticks and I have a bond, there's no denying that. I glance over at Jules, wondering if he's secretly jealous of our weird relationship.

"What about this cute little Tuxedo kitten? Look how fancy he looks!" Jules says softly, petting the cutest baby kitten through the bars of his cage.

"Ask the lady to take him out." I whisper, looking over at the kitten who has now climbed the bars to try to get more attention. "He needs a proper Ahhh Sheebena to see if he's the right one."

Jules glances up at me with a look of pure confusion. "What the fuck did you just say?"

"You have to Lion King him!" I say.

No wonder Fishsticks hates him. He knows nothing about cats.

Throwing my hands up in the air, I mutter, "You have to put him up in the air and do like Rafiki."

"Liam, you have lost your mind," he states, holding the door open to flag down the rescue worker. "But I'm going to do it anyway. I will Ahhh Sheebena that kitten all day long if you let me take him home."

Little does he know, there is no way I could put up a fight. Seeing Jules' eyes full of happiness like this makes me weak in the knees. I could never say no.

After three Ahh Sheebenas and some head boops to Jules' nose, we are now the proud owner of a Tuxedo cat named Theo. I'm not even mad about it. But oh man, Fishsticks is going to lose his shit.

CHAPTER 63

Daily Cat-ffirmation:

I do not have a sense of humor anymore.
It's just sarcasm
and a general hate
for the human population.

Dear Diary,

The humans have returned from their fun filled vacation while I was left with two shrieking and moaning women. They have no idea what I had to put up with while they were away. If I had more self-control, I would have decided to be angry at them for several sunrises. But the love of my new replacement human overrode any possibilities of spiteful revenge.

When I heard my new replacement human cat calling me at the door, I could not have been more delighted. I was finally able to come out of hiding and get the proper attention that I deserve. What I found awaiting me was the worst event in my feline history.

The humans have, again, decided to give me a roommate without my permission. This time of the feline variety, and it is not just any type of feline, it is a small kit. No, they could not afford me the decency of dealing with a grown feline. They had to get a small-boned creature that acts much like a velociraptor.

I immediately expressed my displeasure with several growls and hisses, but the humans did not seem to care about my thoughts on the matter and completely ignored me. They continued to take the tiny barbarian out of its torture chamber to introduce me. I do not need an introduction, what I need is for them to take that thing back where it came from.

I refuse to acknowledge that thing's existence. I just got rid of that witchy woman and her multiple and now the humans pull a stunt like this. I can never win.

These fluffing humans and their fluffing ideas to bring home another fluffing feline. What the fluff? Fluff them. Fluff this world. And fluff my seventh life.

I swear, this is my worst life yet.

CHAPTER 64

Fishsticks

Dear Diary,

I could kill Liam for doing this to me. But then I'd be stuck with Jules. And I fluffing hate Jules.

EPILOGUE

One Year Later-ish

Dear Diary,

It's been three-hundred-sixty-three days and approximately one of my lives since the worst day of my lives.

When Theo, the Tuxedo Cat, came into my habitat I fought back with every ounce of my feline being. The humans in this house used to utter words such as evil, beast, and something about Satan at me during those dark days. I am not sure what those terms mean, but whenever they yelled them, it sounded like they needed to hack up hairballs.

I decided to try harder to alleviate my dissatisfaction with my situation the day I realized I could train the minion to torture the humans out of spite for bringing him into my habitat. I had to work with what I had, even though my situation was unsatisfactory.

I put in long hours training the small kit to do as I commanded. At first, he rebelled against any and all instruction. I spent hours being tormented by him. He continually attempted to bite me, lay on top of my body, and he always chased my feather duster of a tail around the enclosure. He was the epitome of a stage five clinger. I thought that Elon Musk's robotic device was bad! But with hard work and dedication, he soon started picking up on my nonverbal cues.

After eight months of rigorous training, he became the feline I brain-washed him to be. He has now learned to torture the humans in ways that I never even imagined. My favorite skill that he has learned is when he lunges at the humans' heads when they are sleeping. Oh, the joy and delight I get out of watching him cause so much distress.

In the end, this leads to less work for me. I no longer need to expend my energy getting back at the humans for thinking it was wise to bring home this obtuse creature, as I have trained him to do all the work for me.

I am now considered 'the good cat' due to Theo the Tuxedo Cat's behavior, and even though he says that since he is a Tuxedo Cat, and therefore he is fancy, I am the one being treated like royalty. Just as I deserve.

As always, Fishsticks has prevailed.

GLOSSARY
OF CAT TERMS

Bastet: The Egyptian goddess of cats. Known for protection of family, home, and her role in fertility and childbirth. Depicted with a face of a feline.

Biscuits: When a cat massages blankets or a person with their paws. It is often referred to as "making biscuits," due to the similar way that bread makers rhythmically knead dough.

Boop: When a cat touches a human with its nose. In cat language, a boop on the nose by your cat can be the show of belief and trust in a human.

Catio: A place where cats can go outside safely. Also known as: patio.

Daggers: A cat's claws. Also known as: scratchers.

Kitty Condo: A structure for a cat to play, exercise, relax, and sleep on. Also known as: cat tree.

Lion cut: A shaved grooming style that removes most of the hair but leaves the hair on a few small areas. The typical lion cut will leave hair on the face and head, lower half of all four paws, and on the top of the tail which makes them resemble a lion.

Loaf: When a cat tucks themselves into a rectangular shape with their paws beneath them and their tail wrapped around themselves. It is known as a loaf because they resemble a loaf of bread.

Murder Muffins: When a cat makes biscuits on a person aggressively, usually with their claws out.

Orange cat energy: Chaotic behavior akin to that of an orange cat. See also: the "all orange cats share one brain cell" theory.

Paw and Order: Similar to the television show called Law and Order, but feline edition.

Paws-itive: The way a cat says the word positive.

Purrfect: The way a cat says the word perfect.

Scritches: The act of lovingly scratching or petting those hard-to-reach places cats can't get to on their own.

Toe beans: The soft paw pads located on the underside of a cat's paw. It is known as toe beans because of the similarity between the cat's paws and jellybeans.

Fishsticks'

CAT-FFIRMATIONS

In my sadness, I love myself.

I am the perfect size.

The word Anger is just one letter short of Danger.

I refuse to live, laugh, or love.

I am king; therefore, I deserve to be happy.

I am a mighty hunter.

I am a magnificent creature.
Therefore, I am worthy of snacks.

I am thankful for what I once had.

I am getting everything I deserve.

I am the most stunning shade of orange;
therefore, I have orange cat energy.

I am the superior species.

I wouldn't have to manage my anger
if the humans would manage their stupidity.

I am the good-est boy.

I am the best at 10/10 loaves.

No tuna, no peace.

I may not be better than I used to be,
but I am certainly better than
Chuck Norris the Ragdoll in 6C.

Do not dance like no one is watching, because I guarantee some is.

I am glad I am me.

I am royalty and deserve to be treated as such.

This too shall pass,
and then some other stuff will come and take its place.
It never fluffing ends.

I will not let the idiotic behavior of the humans destroy my inner peace.

I know my worth.

When you are royalty,
everything works in your favor.

Even though I am hairless, I am still a handsome feline.

It is better to try and fail, than not try at all.

I do not have a sense of humor anymore.
It's just sarcasm
and a general hate for the human population.

If this is your first book with Fishsticks, you can read more about him in *The Right Wrong Number* by Katie Warren.

DR. THEO

If you'd like to read more about Dr. Theo, look for him in the Sparrow's Nest novels: *Rock Me Gently* and *Loving Out Loud*, by Dianna Roman and Katie Warren.

ACKNOWLEDGEMENTS

Thank you to these wonderful peeps who made this book what it is:

My husband—who came up with so many ideas for this book that his name should be on the cover right beside mine.

Dianna—for dealing with me. There should be a major award for that accomplishment alone.

Kristie (aka: @bookwyrms_shelf)—for reading this as I wrote it. You have no idea how much you helped me keep going.

To my tattoo artist, Govina —for nailing another cover.

To all the readers of *The Right Wrong Number* who pushed me to write a whole book about a deranged orange cat—thank you. This little novella wouldn't be here without you.

I know none of y'all can see it, but I'm doing (another) happy dance right now. It's good. Like a million dollars good, and it's all because of your help. This dance is in your honor, and if you could see it, you'd feel more honored than you ever have before. Or you'd cringe and walk away. Whatever.

ABOUT THE AUTHOR

Katie lives in that thing called a state and rumor has it, in an underground bunker. She has a husband, one of those kid things, and a whole damn farm. She tells her family, “I do what I want,” on a frequent basis and suggests that you do the same.

You can find her over in The Land of Bookstagram as @ katieiscompletelyfine.

Made in United States
Troutdale, OR
03/26/2025